I0545073

EmErika
The Witch, the Wolf
& the Vampire
A.F. Roberts

Em-Erika (The Witch, the Wolf & the Vampire)
First edition. May 30, 2021
Copyright © A.F. Roberts
ISBN: 978-1-7361516-3-1
Written by A.F. Roberts

For Emily & Erica, the real-life cousins who originally inspired this tale

Preface

The formation of this particular tale has proven to be unique in a number of ways.

Its inception – wholly based on two real people who *are* indeed cousins. It's been part of my writing style to incorporate elements of reality into my stories: things from real life, or influences from entertainment; books, movies, television or music. But rarely have I created characters based utterly on actual people I've known, such being the case here. Due to my propensity to play with name-blends, I was taken with how combining the names Emily and Erika equated to 'EmErika,' and how, in pronunciation, it mirrors our country's name.

This made me want to reflect something *of* the US of A *in* the story itself. Perhaps, I thought, some actual American history, which I never dared dream of writing about. Since my bent is toward the supernatural, it occurred to maybe dabble somewhere in the realm of – the Salem Witch Trials? And if, in dealing with a possible witch, why not add a werewolf character, since I already had a two-person name base by merit of the title?

Later still, it struck me that, with this *duo,* why not go for the *trifecta,* and add a *vampire* – considering I'd already created one for the novel *Blood Light.* One whom, by the cannon built in *that* story, was roughly two hundred years old, give or take. Why not 'prequel' her, and explore when she first came to this country from her point-of-origin in England – and have her encounter these two yet-to-be-built characters.

So, the stage was set to do a period piece – my first ever – in my mind, a daunting task. With the two-hundred-year margin previously set by utilizing *Blood Light's* protagonist, going with the Salem timeline was *out* – that would've been one hundred years too early. Thus, I set about looking for American witch history samplings in the late 1700s, which I found existed, but were sparse. Trying to tie into some actual witch tales from that time was cumbersome, so a wholly original storyline proved to be the best course.

What *did* formulate from the historical happenings of that time, however, was the friction between Colonial and Native Americans. There, I mused, would be good fodder for the werewolf character – an Indian – with a wolf 'spirit-animal.' Perfect.

Not only would I be dealing with the spiritual, paranormal side of things, but race as well; a dark time indeed for racial relations in this land. Not really a subject I wanted to tackle, but this was the general time sequence I'd stuck myself with, so I set out to portray the subject with the care and conscious I believe it is due. Overall, I'm surprised and pleased with how well the narrative turned out; the depth of characterizations I was able to achieve – and the highly sympathetic characters of these two noble young women – *Emily* and *Erika*.

Also 'cheers,' as the English say, to *Charissa* (the vampire) as well!

– *A.F.*

Prologue
Tennessee, 1778

For unto them, this day, to this tribe was born a daughter – to a woman of the native heritage, and to a man who was not. In the eighteenth century's blending of peoples both indigenous *and* transplanted to the Americas, yet another couple had formed from contrasting cultures. As always with territories where one race was first and a second came for conquest, nothing was easy and conflict came before peace. So it was with Jed and Taynee (meaning born during the return of the moon); who named their new girl Erika, Jed's preference.

Their respective kinsmen and tribesmen were not accepting of them in the beginning; though in time, *the tribe* acknowledged the white man once his honor was proven and his loyalty to Taynee was clear. Such *was not* the case with Jed's brother, Robert. He continued to refute his sibling's choice of mate, ultimately shunning Jed from his life and his family, the Laydons.

Chapter 1
Emily

As it so happened, Robert and his wife Kate likewise *already* had a young daughter prior to this, who they named Emily. Robert Laydon was a colonial puritan Christian man, while Kate, entirely unbeknownst to her husband, *had* been a practicing – witch. So fully in love had she fallen with Robert that she'd simply made the choice – to renounce the magic. For she knew, being the man he was, combined with the days and territory in which they lived, that the two *could not* co-exist. Thus, she married him and hung up the practice for love. Though the customs of the time might have dictated to do so, Kate could not bring herself to destroy her grimoires; she simply packed and buried them deep within their basement, so to never be found. Or so she thought. She could pack and bury, stop practicing, deny herself; but one fact remained – she was inherently a creature of magic – and so too by descent, would be her offspring.

• • • •

Emily and Erika were two and a half years and perhaps twenty miles apart, from the colonial settlement to the Indian territory. That distance nor Robert's mandate not to see Jed could stop Emily from becoming aware of Erika's birth when it came.

Before that though, up until she was one and a half, she knew Jed while he was still around. Before a government job as an 'peace agent' into Indian land under George Washington would see him reside among Taynee's Chickasaw village, and she would fall in love with him, and he with her.

Even at the tender age of only two, Emily was dreaming immediately of her cousin's fresh presence into the world when it came about, following Jed and Taynee's union.

The mind of the child could not know what any of it meant; to her it simply *was,* and wasn't anything out of the ordinary as far as she was concerned. If anything *was* unusual to Emily, it was Jed's absence. As time and years advanced, *he* was beginning to show up more and more in her dreams of the Indian baby girl. Likewise, little Erika began to see Emily vividly in her own dreams also.

This combination of elements, the dreamt cohesion of Jed and Erika together at last prompted Emily to verbalize to her parents what she was seeing and feeling. At this point, she was four years old.

"Momma," she would ask, "why is Unca' Jed with my baby friend and not 'round here na'more?"

Taken aback, Kate hesitantly replied, "Honey, you *know* Jed took a job that sent him away. Remember?" she reminded, trying to fish out where this was coming from and where it could be going.

"I 'member. But I think he wants to come back now. He's with the brown baby girl. She tell me he's done his job. He should come home."

"Em, you have a baby Indian friend? Where is she? How do you see her?"

"When I sleep, Mommy!"

Kate gasped, taking her hand to cup her mouth. Knowing where Jed actually was, *who* he'd come to be with, and doing the logical math, she knew what Em had discovered.

In her dreams.

By *magical* intuition.

Jed had had a daughter! And somehow, Emily knew it. Somehow, by the inherited witch gene from Kate, Emily had a dream power to see the truth.

Kate had prayed that this day would never come – and worried for when it did. When Robert's lies to Em to cover his intolerance for where Jed actually was, and why he wasn't coming back was finally catching up, and Em was catching on. She wasn't fully there yet, but Kate saw that, in this, it was beginning.

Fearful of the potential for so much to unravel and her past biting her in the behind, Kate pulled Emily close, hugging her hard. "Em, whenever you want to talk about the baby girl or Uncle Jed, you talk *to me* – do you understand? Only me! Your father wouldn't understand these things of dream. But I do, and I will hear you. I will understand. Talk to *me*. Do you hear me?" she asked sternly, pulling Em back from her hold to look her in the eyes.

"I un'stand, Momma," Emily replied. "Just you, na Daddy. I will. Promise."

Kate pulled her back close again and cradled her. She knew she was making the best decision she could, given the circumstances, to confide *only* in her. Unfortunately, in excluding the young girl from speaking

to her father on the subject, Kate was also creating a dividing line that would one day ultimately polarize Robert and Emily in ways she could not even dream of now. But, when faced with the stark reality of really *no* good choices to make, what's a mother to do?

· · · ·

As the weeks ensued after Emily's initial reveal of her dreams to Kate, things quieted down. The daughter kept her promise to her mother with regard to speaking of it. Emily would offer little snippets of Erika getting bigger, learning to walk and say her first words. Of particular interest was how Emily was somehow translating to English what Erika would say in Native dialect.

Kate was amazed at the clarity and involvement with which Emily was able to interact with the girl in her dreams. It was almost as if she were there in person, engaging with the family, seeing her cousin's growth. She felt a certain joy and pride in her daughter's prowess to do this; yet simultaneously felt a growing bitterness towards Robert's bigotry that was forcing Em to experience it all in this fashion, rather than in *real life*.

Both presently and as more time passed, Kate found herself longing to speak to Robert of these things, as any wife wants to share the happenings of life with her husband. But she could not, any more than she could have her ever-growing daughter talk with him about it. It was two-fold and too much. First, the mystery and wonder of the dreamworld would likely be misconstrued by Robert's puritan paranoia as witchcraft; which was still alive and well regardless of nearly a hundred years passing since the witch trials of Salem. Second,

if the former *were* spoken of, it could begin the slippery slope leading to a reveal of Kate actually being one. Imagine! If he was put off this much by a woman merely of a different color, God only knew how he'd react to his own wife keeping secret that she was a *witch!* Never mind that she no longer practiced!

Sadly, these conversations couldn't, *mustn't* ever be brokered.

Chapter 2
Erika

A village of the Chickasaw Nation where Jed and Taynee dwelt, lay southwest of where Emily lived in the outskirts of Clarksville, between the Big Sandy and Tennessee Rivers. At the time, Indian Territory took up the larger portion of the state, though that would change drastically within a few decades. The main tribes of Tennessee were the Chickasaw and Cherokee. There had been others, such as the Shawnee and Yuchi, but they had since departed, moving north and south respectively, during the course of the last hundred years.

One day when Erika was two-and-a-half-going-on-three, Jed and Taynee awoke early, while Erika slept on. Unlike Kate's situation with Robert, Taynee shared openly with Jed things young Erika had spoken to her of regarding – dreams.

"It is amazing," said Taynee, snuggling up close to Jed, "what Erika has been telling me of – that which she dreams of."

"Yes?" asked Jed, brushing her hair. "Remembering her dreams already, even so young? That *is* remarkable."

"It might just be," Taynee answered. "I can't be sure of course, but I believe she's been trying to say that she's seeing this other girl when she sleeps. A young white girl. Moreover, she seems to be speaking of seeing a man *with* the girl too. He's not there much, just a little, she says – and that he looks kind of like you! And there's a woman also, probably the mother, I'd guess."

Jed had been somewhat puzzled as to what she was telling to him – up until she got to that last part. *A man who looked like himself* **with** *a young, white* **girl**. Erika was dreaming of Emily, Robert and Kate! His eyes opened wide as he shot up from his place of rest beside Taynee.

"What is it, my *hattak*?" she asked, calling him husband.

"She's dreaming of my niece and my brother, Tanyee! That has to be what it is! But how in Sam Hill does she dream them when she doesn't even *know* of them – since Robert *won't* see us?"

Tanyee smiled at Jed knowingly, caressing his cheek as she replied, "She's reaching out *beyond* the known – and learning of that which is hidden to her. She cannot know the girl – Emily – you say? Because of Robert's obstinance, this cousin remains veiled to her. But Erika is pushing past his rigidness and learning of her through the dreamworld."

"Do you think Em dreams of her too?" asked Jed, curious as to his wife's thoughts.

"Is she a special child?" Taynee offered back with a question for a question.

"Why yes," he answered, "she's very exceptional!"

"Well then, I think she just might," concluded Taynee. "Who might – wha?" exclaimed their now-awake and fully-energized daughter, suddenly bounding into their space, sandwiching herself between them.

Taynee pulled her close and snuggled Erika, answering her directly, having no sense of need to hide their conversation in any way. To do so was not the Chickasaw way. "The girl you dream about, wolf girl!" She called her this because Erika was born early in the month of March, making the girl's spirit animal the wolf, according to the Chickasaw.

"I was telling your *inki* (father) about your friend from your dreams, and we wondered if she might dream of you too?"

"Yea!" Erika cried with enthusiasm, "she do – we talk!"

"So, if you talk, then you also *walk*," her mother continued, "**dream**-*walk* with her!"

Erika furrowed her nose at her mother, not understanding, as did Jed.

Tanyee looked at both of them intently and said, "Close your eyes, both of you, and keep them closed." As the two acquiesced, she gently took each of their heads in both her hands, slowly moving them together so they touched. "With your eyes closed now, pretend your sleeping – and dreaming – together. It's like you're *walking* with each other in the dream. *Dream-walking.*"

Having taken her direction in the brief exercise, they both imagined themselves together, walking hand-in-hand. They got it, unconsciously smiling in unison, which remained as they opened their eyes once more. Taynee grinned back in satisfaction to both their smiles as well as having helped them understand.

To this, Erika added more to her already formidable enthusiasm by suggesting, "Me and Inki should dream to my friend and *her* Inki together!"

Jed and Taynee exchanged a look of apprehension to one another, both knowing full well that any attempt to pull Robert into an Indian dream world where his brother and his native girl were was a bad idea.

Jed was about to speak to the point, but Taynee got there first; and being more knowledgeable on the subject, he was grateful not to have to fumble through redirecting his daughter. *"Pushkush,* (daughter) no, that would be very hard to do. Trying to make dreams with a lot of people together isn't easy. It takes much practice and focus. Just keep dreaming to your friend. Maybe try to dream to Inki. But keep it to one person at a time. Perhaps when you're older you can try with more."

Erika listened to her intently, scrutinizing the advice. Apparently satisfied that her mother had her best interest at heart, she replied, "Okay *Ishki,* (mother) I will. Just Inki or my friend." Then she hugged Tanyee and Jed respectively and scurried away to play with her siblings.

The two parents sighed relief in unison as to the bullet they'd dodged with respect to the ever-problematic Robert and his incessant bigotry. They too hugged each other, falling into a restful, sustained embrace.

• • • •

Chapter 3

Charissa

London, 1783 – My name is Charissa Westcott of Farringdon. I have dark hair with an olive complexion, was raised as a good middle class Catholic girl and brought up right. I went to a church-run girls' school through my formative years, learning literature, history, geography, science, foreign language and religion. I was lucky my parents could afford this luxury, because, being female, there was always the stronger emphasis upon the 'dame schooling' of sewing, painting and music – the more accepted station of women; that of simply becoming a wife. Though my parents *did* wish me successfully married off, I believe they also wanted me smarter and more well-rounded than what the times called for a woman to be. I never questioned my upbringing in any way and believed wholly that how I was being molded was absolutely right and proper.

I'm a young lady of twenty now, though with what I've endured over the last several years and the conclusion thereof, I feel much older. Following the natural, expected course, when I was about sixteen, I'd begun seeing a boy two years my elder, James. He, being all of eighteen at the time, should I have called him a boy or a man? Hard to say and entirely irrelevant. In the end, he proved himself to be little more than a child regardless.

James was from a good family as well, but was something of a black-sheep, I'd come to find. He'd feigned interest in the faith, but I think only to appeal to my good graces. This worked for a while, but his true goal, to know me intimately, in time began to override all else. I'd always been clear that I'd sought to wait for marriage. I had no hiccups on my ledger previous to him – I was pure – and had every intention to stay that way. He, conversely, had other ideas. He was patient at first, and for good while I must credit – a couple of years actually. But once he'd crossed the threshold of twenty, something changed. He wanted to feel like a *man*.

I, on the other hand, being only eighteen at that point, still felt like a girl, not yet a woman. I dared convention to focus on the studies of my higher education rather than the contemplation of marriage and family. And to me, *that was* synonymous with sexual encounters. Our *first* encounter, in terms of introduction, was at university where he was in his second year while I was in my last – of secondary school. Those in year thirteen sometimes got to visit a college to scout their future schooling, and so it was with 'lucky me' from *my* school. We had a chance meeting that day on campus during a break in the tour; followed by a not-so-chance rendezvous at a college party, my invitation by him. From that point, we only saw each other randomly through the remainder of the school year, then summer, still only connecting periodically, to my parents' chagrin. It wasn't until we were both attending *together* the following year when things really began to take off.

And take off it did. It was magical in the beginning – fun, passionate, exciting! I am not one to be swept away, but before too long I found myself indeed falling for him. He was headstrong, ambitious and admittedly good potential as a husband. Despite all that, I resisted moving along too quickly in the relationship. I was raised a proper lady and I wanted it to go at a slow and steady pace. And I wished it that way for far longer than he was prepared for it to be. My continued persistence to a long courtship would ultimately be the catalyst for where things would go quite wrong.

A little past the year mark in our courting was when James's patience with me began to run out. He started, on certain occasions, trying to force himself on me. A time or two I almost gave in, but in the end, I forced him away, frustrating and maddening him all the more. Then came the time when no amount of 'no's' nor strength on my part would dissuade him. He'd almost defiled me when, somehow, I managed to pull away, then kick him in the groin with all my might. Obviously, it stopped him for *that* incident, but as time went on, I thought I may have done some real damage. When I'd pass him afterwards upon campus, his gait was off as though he were compensating, perhaps, for the injury. I couldn't verify as he would no longer talk to me, let alone see me. It appeared as though we were over. And yet...

And yet, it *wasn't* the case, as time would tell. It didn't happen overnight by any means, of course. There were hurt feelings as well as body parts that had to heal. But in time, those hurts and awkwardness between us subsided. Distance and disdain for one another eased as we continued to see each other in passing at school. Frowns and furrowed brows were eventually replaced again by mutual grins here and there. And finally, a grin would turn to a smile or a look of yearning. I didn't know why or how it was happening after what had previously occurred, it just *was*.

Chapter 4
Emily

Several years had now passed and Emily had reached the ripe old age of seven. As tended to happen with 'imaginary friends' and age, the vivid dreams of Erika had diminished to a great extent. It wasn't that they never occurred anymore, they simply didn't happen near as much, nor were they as interactive.

It was hard to pinpoint exactly when the shift took place; but Kate was very attuned to it when it came about. It was about the time when Emily was old enough to assume chores and her schooling began. The addition of these elements of 'real life' began pushing her previous, more idle mind away from the journeys of imagination. Or at least, these were Kate's general ideas of what had happened. In any event, she simply knew that Emily was speaking to her less of Erika and Jed and more of schoolwork and help with her chores. It wasn't, of course, that they had no slaves for the work as Tennessee *was* a southern state; but both parents felt that their child needed to learn a solid work ethic.

So, though Kate missed the talks and learning things of Erika and the estranged family, she was relieved that the powers making it all possible were subsiding. Powers which were an ever-present threat of exposure to Robert, a danger to them both.

Kate was not foolhardy enough to assume that nothing else would ever manifest again, however. Though she wasn't looking back with regret that she'd given up the practice, she *did* recall her own coming-of-age and growth into her powers. Presumably, she would likely have to contend with it happening to Emily too, at some point. But for the time being, all was well. But it wouldn't be long till this also would shift.

Before long, it came to pass that Robert decided Emily should learn to hunt with him. It wasn't that Robert had some great, deep yearning to have a son – he simply felt that *any* child of his should know how to shoot and hunt. It actually proved to be a good bonding experience for them both. Unfortunately, because of the general area they'd traverse, it would also begin to create a festering sore between them as well.

Case in point, early on into one of their excursions, they'd tracked a deer which bolted off from them – in the *wrong* direction. Emily moved to give chase, but Robert stopped her from going. Perplexed, Emily asked, "Why, Daddy?"

"Because, darling," he replied, "going further that way will take us into Indian lands, and we don't want to go there."

"Why not?" she continued to press. "The Chickasaw are a friendly tribe, aren't they? Besides, that's where Uncle Jed went to live, right?"

"What do *you* know about it, Emily?" he retorted. "Friendly or not, we don't go around the Indians. And Jed should never have gotten as 'friendly' as he did with them. That wasn't his job. He was just supposed to do 'race relations,' not marry one of them!"

And there it was. Whether unwittingly or deliberate, Robert had unleashed his hard line against both their native neighbors *and* his brother, all in one fell swoop. And to Emily, it was like a punch in the gut. Being early into the hunting experience, it was too soon for her to tell whether she liked it or not. But she knew she *didn't like* her father's attitude towards the natives, nor her uncle. Regardless, she didn't pursue it further and kept her mouth shut – for Robert had spoken, in no uncertain terms.

So, they then moved off into another direction. Robert continued giving instruction of the hunt to Emily, but not a great deal was said beyond that. She remained more subdued the rest of the day with thoughts of Jed and Erika dredged up because of what Robert had said. As this day of hunting ended, she told herself that she would try to dream of them more again.

As the days and weeks passed, Emily found that she'd lost, or at least misplaced, her knack for dreaming to them like she did when she was younger. Try as she might, she could not get them to come as they used to. Frustrated but not dissuaded, she determined to try, somehow, to get into Chickasaw land, try to find them herself, while on the hunt with Robert. It wouldn't be easy – it would take skill, scheming and a lot of distraction to pull off, but that was okay. She had time, patience and opportunity – and she was going to make the best of it.

Time pushed on with Emily's hunting and shooting skills improving, but they still weren't great. Surprisingly, Robert's patience to this was steadfast, and he remained diligent with her. He never got angry, even if she wasn't progressing as fast as he might like. In his mind he

probably chalked it up to her being female, not being as natural at it

like she would've if she'd been a boy. He saw too, that she was engaged and making a good effort. Little did he know that her *main* interest in the pastime was that it got them closer to the land which was her goal to get into. Still, exactly how to do it while she was out with Robert *and* be able to deviate away to find her true quarry remained unclear. Since he would not go there, nor allow her to, separating themselves would be a must. But again, *how?*

One night before bed as Emily was saying her prayers, an idea occurred. It seemed as though in answer to the many prayers she'd already placed, asking God for help to meet her ends. It finally struck her that, before her father had started taking her, he'd sometimes take one of the slaves out with him on a hunt. What if she could convince him to have *two* of them along, so that they might cover more ground – in *pairs?* That way, she'd not be alone while slinking away to Chickasaw territory and apart from him. And *he'd* be distracted enough being with another as well. Would he even allow her to be with one of them by themselves, and *not* with him? Clearly, the only way to find out would be to simply ask, *and* improve enough in skill so he'd trust her more to be with someone else besides him. The trick was – to find a way to present the notion without it sounding suspect. Why on God's green earth would she even think of such a thing unless she was up to no good?

Emily needed help with this – and just as before when it came to things of Erika and Jed, she would confide to the only one she could in the matter – her mother. Mom might help if she knew what she was trying to accomplish. And Kate could have an idea how to appeal to

her Dad's better sense. It was worth a try, as long as it didn't

compromise Mother's standing with Robert – too much. Moreover, Emily determined to play it smart and draw her Mom *to* herself, rather than *she* going to Kate.

This played out in the following fashion one day when Emily and Robert returned from hunting practice: Kate greeted her daughter and asked "How did it go today, sweetheart?"

Emily silently shrugged a bit, stalling for Robert to kiss Kate hello, then retire to change clothes. She spoke up after he was gone and said, "It's going good, Mom. I like it a lot – but not for the reason Father thinks. I mean, the hunting's fine – but the real reason I like it out there is that it gets us close to Chickasaw land. And I want to go there! But naturally, that's out of the question as far as he's concerned. You *know* why I want to go there, yes?"

"Of course," Kate answered apprehensively.

"You know I've lost the dreams, right? The ones where I could see them – be with them?"

"I know. And that's why you want to physically go there now. *Very* risky, daughter."

"*I know,* Mom, of course it is. Almost impossible. But I have a plan. I won't tell you much of it, because I don't want to get *you* in any trouble. Only this – I'm going to need Ben and Isaiah to go with us sometimes, so we can split up in pairs out there. I'm telling you this because I need your advice on how to ask him about it in a way that will make sense."

"Out of something that makes almost no sense!" Kate snapped. "Any ideas I have to help you I should absolutely keep to myself, Em. But – I

know your heart's in the right place in what you seek. And out of

respect to the promise you've always kept – speaking only to me of Jed and your cousin – I *will* offer you what little I can. And that is this: Find a way to make your father think it's *his* idea. As far as a good reason to have help out there and the *need* to be in pairs; tell him you've been thinking ahead about stocking up on game for the winter. He'll like the initiative. He used to take them out hunting with him before he began training you, so that will be a natural segue."

"*That's* how I got the idea, Mom – from them being the first to hunt with him."

"You're getting to be a smart one, aren't you Emily? And you're going to have to be *real* smart to pull this off and not have it explode in your face! How are you progressing in your hunting skill? That's going to be very key in his allowing you to be with somebody else, you know."

"Yes, I know, Mom. I've thought about that, and I'm getting better. I'll start practicing my shooting every day. And I won't even bring up the idea till he sees how good I'll get. Because, unless he *does,* he won't even consider taking the boys."

"Exactly," Kate replied, beckoning her daughter to come in for a hug. "Don't make me regret this," she continued, holding Emily close. "Be smart, be cunning, be wise, daughter. But more than anything, once you commit, be *ready*. You hear me, Em?"

"I hear you, Mom. Thank you for your help. When the time comes, I promise – *I'll be ready.*"

• • • •

Chapter 5

Erika

A round this same time, another was getting herself 'ready' as well. Young Erika, though only a little over five now, wasn't considered by any means *too young* to also begin hunting. For this was an indigenous tribe, hunter gatherers by nature, not Americanized English who treated hunting as more of a pastime – it was a way of life. As such, the children learned early.

Erika took to it like second nature – eager, willing, and quite a natural with the bow. Accuracy took some time, but within the year, she was shooting, literally, straight as an arrow. Beyond that, it proved to be a combined learning and bonding experience for both her and Jed.

Jed was instructed out-of-the-gate along with her as his only hunting experience was naturally, with a gun. Wanting to participate but not interfere, he welcomed learning the Chickasaw ways of the hunt right there with his daughter as she came into her own. So too did he, and together they became a formidable duo. A far more in-sync pair than their counterparts, Emily and Robert; who, for as much as they enjoyed themselves together, would never be as unified of mind as their relatives – for obvious reasons.

One day when they'd hunted entirely on their own, they'd wandered a bit further than normal, pushing towards the colonists' territory. At six and a half now, Jed felt utterly confident in Erika's skills and didn't mind letting her briefly out of his sight, if the hunt necessitated it. Between themselves, they weren't sure *exactly* which direction their quarry had moved. One thought this way, and the other that way. Thus, they split up so as to be certain that whichever way, one of them would be on the trail.

As it turned out, Erika had been right, and shortly spotted the deer in the distance. Suddenly, as she had her bow pulled and readied, she felt that she'd been 'spotted' herself. The feeling of eyes upon her, of being watched. By someone familiar, something connected to her. Man? Animal? Erika's mind quickly recollected her birth month and what animal that represented, as well of the meaning of her mother's name, *born at the moon,* simultaneously. "Beast?" she called out – to nothing. No creature was there that she could tell.

In the instant she'd made noise, her prey reacted and took to run. She whirled to get off a shot; not so much to land it, but to get the animal more directed to where she knew Jed was. "Inki!" she shouted this time, "coming to you!" His reactions were timely and on the mark. By the time Erika had returned to him, he'd felled the deer. They smiled knowingly to one another, proud of themselves for the good team they'd become. He hoisted her up in his arms to bask in the moment, fully aware he wouldn't be able to treat her this way too much longer. They snuggled nose-to-nose for a minute before Erika reminded him, "Inki, the deer," nodding downward that they should attend to it. Yes, she was growing up fast!

He set Erika down, and both she and Jed immediately moved to their fallen deer, first to make sure it was fully deceased, then to pray over it, thanking it for its sacrifice – the Chickasaw way. After which Jed hauled it up over his shoulder to carry to their horses farther away, where one could take the deer's burden and the other, the two riders as they returned to village.

In the course of their trek back, Erika noticed something out of the corner of her eye. No, it *wasn't* the sense of being watched again, but rather the progress of something else moving parallel to them as they rode. Something bigger than say, a rabbit, but smaller than the deer carcass they had in tow. Upon closer observation, she surmised it to be a stray wolf cub apart from the pack it should've been with. She poked Jed to get his attention to it, but he was wary to approach. She begged him to stop, pleading her case that this had to do with her 'animal spirit,' which he was fairly well aware of. He acquiesced, but only to come to a halt, at least initially.

Soon they could see that the cub had stopped also, further garnering Erika's interest in it. And then it came as he regrettably anticipated: "Please Inki, let me down?" She wanted to *go* to the wolf, naturally. Jed looked around for as far as he could see, looking for any signs of the rest of the pack. Seeing none, he sighed, easing himself down off their horse, then gathering Erika to himself, pulling her off as well. He'd seriously hoped the beast would then leave, startled away by their movement off the equine. But of course, it *didn't,* the wolf remained static as if, inexplicably, waiting for *her.*

Damn the luck, Jed thought. Now, more than likely, he'd have to see this through. And sure enough, Erika pointed toward the deer, indicating to cut a piece of it off that she could take in offering to the animal. Sighing again, he brought out his blade and sliced away a goodly chunk of deer meat. No sooner had he sheathed *that* weapon, he pulled out another – his pistol. He was not about to let this scenario go astray, should things go south of his daughter's intentions. He silently pointed to his eyes that he was keeping a close watch, simultaneously unlocking the gun's safety so that she knew he was prepared if this endeavor went sideways. She nodded back in understanding. She didn't like it, but was the best she could hope for given how wide a berth he was giving her.

Slow and steady she approached the wolf, ready with an offering any predator should appreciate. As she neared him, she could see he was probably seven to nine months old. Jed was not close enough to make the age determination as he held back, so as to not spook the animal while Erika attempted to make friends with it. Still, he was near enough for a true shot if it proved necessary.

All this while, the wolf had not come closer, but neither had it retreated in any way. She *had* his attention. Erika crouched down in a passive stance, outstretching her arm with the deer meat in hand. She not only had his attention, but his interest as well. Finally, he advanced towards her while Jed took in a sharp breath of anticipation. The wolf was within arm's reach now, sniffing the air in front of him, taking in Erika's scent – and that sumptuous smell of a fresh kill. At last he took her gift, his snout gently nibbling it out of her hand. He consumed it with satisfaction and was ready for more. Erika produced an

additional chunk from her other hand which he gladly took from her. As he chewed away on that one, she dug into her side bag for the extra she'd had the foresight to bring along.

So far it was going well. But this was the easy part. To reach her goal and truly make a connection with the animal would be the hard part. Having finished everything she had to give, he just stared at her as if looking for more. She opened up empty hands to show 'all gone.' "That's all I have, boy. See?" she said, lowering one hand, but keeping the other up in friendly gesture to him.

He continued to sniff toward her, then ever so slowly, smell *at* the hand. In the background, Jed sturdied himself for action.

Then it came. Having fully sniffed her out, his nose touched her hand, and he accepted her touch as she moved to pet him. "That's a good boy," said Erika, smiling broadly to his acceptance of her. "Where's your pack, boy? You shouldn't be alone like this." Almost as if in understanding, he let out a lonely whine and nuzzled at her. He started licking her hand, getting the last residues of the deer odor from her fingers onto his palette. Jed stood down from his readied stance, but remained wary.

Not quite sure what do next, Erika began to rise slowly to her feet. As she did, the wolf circled round her legs, bumping at them affectionately as dogs will do with their bonded humans. She pet his head again from her now fully standing position, turning to look towards Jed as if preparing to return to him. At this, the wolf ever so slightly nipped at her hand, pricking a small amount of blood. "Oww," she uttered, recoiling just a bit. "It's okay, I'm just going back to my Inki, boy. Want to come with?" He clearly *did,* following closely as she walked back to her father, again sniffing the air which continued to carry the tantalizing smell of more deer.

While the wolf's hunger drive was foremost on his mind, the small bite from him was on Erika's. She examined the bite mark on her finger as she returned to Jed, fanaticizing that maybe some kind of 'blood-bond' would now be formed between them, solidifying their link.

Jed interrupted her reverie, shouting out, "Did he *bite* you, Erika?" ready to resume to action and chase the wolf away.

"No, it's fine, Inki," she replied, "just a little nip. I don't think he wanted me to come back yet; thought I was going to leave him. I – hey!" she exclaimed, seeing her new friend making a beeline towards the horse carrying the dead deer. Taking immediate alpha authority over a 'pack' subordinate, she quickly bolted in front of the horse, blocking the wolf's advance. Arms crossed and dead serious, she commanded, "No! No more for you right now! The rest is for our tribe. You'll have the scraps and bones when all have had their fill, but not before! You may return with us to the village and receive your due *afterwards.* Do you understand me?"

Whether any animal *truly* understands human speech, the wolf nonetheless bowed down and sat in front of her at her bold orders. Though Jed had initially raised his chin at her notion of the wolf's return with them, he said nothing, impressed beyond words at his daughter's command of the situation *and* of the wolf itself.

And so it went; Jed and Erika mounted again upon their steed, the second horse with the deer in trail to the rear, and the wolf to their side, all forging along at a steady pace in their return to the village beyond the Tennessee River.

Chapter 6

Charissa

ondon, 1784 – So it was that James and I had gotten back on course with one another inexplicably, many months after the incident where he practically raped me. Perhaps my feelings of guilt for injuring him so in my own defense played a part in allowing him another chance. Maybe *he* had learned his lesson. Or there was the chance that we both just started feeling like our old selves again and had simply put the past behind us. Whatever the case, beyond reason and logic, we'd returned to being a couple once more, and all seemed right with the world.

Now as it so happened, during the interim of our time apart, I'd struck up an association-turned-friendship with another upper classmen, also around James' age. She was named Andrea, and proved to be a very thoughtful, highly intelligent girl. We'd met in philosophy class where I'd struggled initially, finding it difficult to mingle my religious views with some of the more worldly ones that were the course's subject matter. Andrea carried a more esoteric mindset herself, and as such, was able to help me navigate through it all much better. This led to many deep and thoughtful conversations between ourselves, far beyond the class content. Before long, we'd become practically inseparable. I'd most assuredly made a girlfriend!

Thus, Andrea and I had become well-established by the time James and I had gotten back together. As such, he was interjected into her presence along with mine; *not that* he didn't know her already, being of the same class level as she. They seemed to get on well with each other, which was good, seeing as how I was their common denominator. It would do me little good if they were conflicted when I liked them both equally.

In time, we became something of a trio, being together oftentimes for meals or events or just co-mingling. And for the course of the next year or so, university life seemed utterly grand to me. I had a boyfriend, a girlfriend, and was learning beyond my wildest dreams! Literally, because most *girls* didn't get this kind of educational opportunity. I'd reached a place of being so fully enamored with my lot in this life – that I'd become entirely oblivious to possible cracks in its armor.

A suspicion to such finally struck me one night when we were all having dinner together at a restaurant. Between the main course and dessert, I'd excused myself to the ladies' room to freshen up. Andrea had not come with me, as she'd been in mid-conversation with James, which was fine, I'd not thought anything of it. Upon my return, however, I couldn't help but notice them from a distance seeming ridiculously comfortable with each other. I'd seen this many times previous, and it was perfectly normal. In this isolated instance though, it seemed to stab at me unnaturally. I didn't know what was happening. Had a veil just been unsheathed from my eyes to reveal what had been right in front of me for a while?

I wasn't sure what to do, and thank God they hadn't seen me yet. I needed a moment to catch my breath from this before returning to the table. Finally, I'd sturdied myself and went back to them, reinserting myself into the mix. James gave me a very nice kiss as I sat, which seemed to settle me down more. Within minutes, all was back to our usual banter, and my sudden lucid moment appeared to be fading into the background. As we wound down with dessert, I realized that this may very well have been the first time I'd ever seen James and Andrea apart from my being *with* them. And when I put it in that perspective, I felt rather silly for the notion of anything amiss.

But silly or not, it proved to be something I couldn't let go no matter how hard I tried. The more I thought about it, the more I was able to make a solid case for them being together. Or, at the very least, James being with *someone* during our break, considering that it was my withholding sex from him that was the crux of our split in the first place, not that *I* was in the wrong for that. Additionally, he'd been nothing but a gentleman now, not pushing me for anything along those lines, and seemingly all right with it presently. This would speak towards him getting it somewhere if he weren't bothering *me* about it any longer. Yes, people *can* change, but so too, tigers don't change their stripes.

So, one day I simply came out with it and talked to him about it. At first, naturally, he was defensive to it, exclaiming, "How could you think that? I wouldn't do that to you," he'd said. Gently, I reminded him of our stained past and how he very nearly took me by force. I pointed out that, if his sex drive was so strong that he'd attempted such against my will, surely he would've satisfied himself with someone while we were apart. And to this, he was forthright and admitted it was so.

"I *was* with another girl, Charissa," said James, "but it wasn't Andrea. I didn't court her, I simply knew her."

"Knew her because she's the same year as you," I offered.

"Yes," he concluded, "because we're in the same class. I've only gotten to know her now because you two are friends. Apart from that, I wouldn't know her any better than I did before. We get along well, so what of it? *You* are my girl – again."

"And so I am. I'm sorry, I was just checking. It's been bothering me lately, since that night at dinner when she remained with you while I freshened up. As I'd returned, I saw you both getting on so well in my absence, it made me wonder. I'd never observed the two of you separate from me like that before, and I guess my imagination ran a little wild. Please forgive me."

He took my hand, kissed it, and said comfortingly, "Nothing to forgive, it's understandable. Now, no more of this talk, eh?"

"No," I agreed, "it shall go no further."

But it did.

. . . .

Weeks later, after I *had* gotten my suspicions under control for the most part, a night came that would prove quite pivotal for Andrea and I. She had stayed over at my dorm after dinner and studying. As girls will do on a sleep over, we shared the bed. Sometime in the middle of the night I awoke, catching myself in the midst of an odd observance. Inadvertently, I perceived in the air a scent that I swore smelled like – James. *What?* I thought to myself. Not really wanting to, but needing to

prove to myself it wasn't just my imagination, I leaned over and began smelling the sleeping Andrea. I am no type of supernatural creature like a vampire or anything, but a keen sense of smell did allow me to detect a faint whiff of my boyfriend. On her! This could be only circumstantial evidence at best of course, but in my mind, it would seem as though someone's probably been lying to me!

At that moment, Andrea also awoke, catching me red-handed in mid-sniff.

"What *ever* are you doing, Charissa?" she asked.

"Um, er, I smelled something good as I woke," I began, fumbling for something plausible, "and found that it was coming from you," I finished.

"Uh huh," she replied, as if not believing me. "Well, if *this* is what you're into, then it might explain a few things; such as why you've been holding out on James."

"What? No! I'm *not* 'into' anything!" I cried. "And I'm not 'holding out.' I've told you why that's a sore spot with us, what he tried to do."

"Yes, I know. I also know that it was because you were doing the same thing prior to *that,* not giving him what he wanted."

"Is that what it's all about? What *he* wants? What about me? What about what *I* want – or don't?"

"Yes, what about you, Charissa? What do *you* want?" she asked somewhat seductively, sniffing me back in close proximity, running her nose up my neck. "Do you want – *me,* perhaps?"

Oh God, I'd gotten myself in deep now. It was becoming crystal clear that she indeed *was* into such as this. My suspiciousness had seemingly gotten me into a situation of my own making. I was about to push her

off when it occurred that if I allowed her to continue a bit, she might go on to reveal something that might give her *and* James away. So I went with it – for as long as I could tolerate.

She turned up her nose now so that her lips eased up my neckline, gently moving towards my chin and mouth. "You know, you might consider *this,* **combined** with being with James. I could help you through it, and guide you out of your inhibitions – it could be fun!"

"And if I *considered* neither?" I retorted, beginning to ease away from her, growing too uncomfortable to continue. Damn whatever I was hoping to get out of her!

"Then you're a fool, Charissa!" she chided. "I don't know if you're scared of intimacy or just a prude, but you'd do yourself a favor if you would simply get over it! Being physical *is* an inherent part of a relationship."

"So, I should not wait for marriage even if it's my preference, you're saying?"

"Not if you want to hold onto James – no! You're half way to losing him already, because as you probably already suspect, he *is* receiving gratification on the side in lieu of what you still *will not* do for him."

"You could only know this in one of two ways, Andrea. Either he's confided in you about it, or – "

"*Or* I'm the one who's taking care of him, Charissa! Yes, for God's sake, it's me! Me and him behind your back! But not anymore, because I'm tired of it! Tired of doing this little dance. Be honest, you weren't getting a whiff of me because 'I smelled good,' but because you thought you smelled *him* on me, isn't that right?"

"Absolutely *right,* my 'friend'!" I barked. "How – how could you?"

"Oh, stop it!" she retaliated. "I *am* being a better friend – to *both* of you – by just admitting it! Even though, I suspect, I will likely lose you both *by* coming out with it."

"Or you could have not done it in the first place," I offered simply.

"*Or* that, of course. Alas, too late for that now, I'm afraid. I think I helped you live in your little dream world for a time; but honestly, though I genuinely like him and think he's a decent man – he's still a *typical* man, and *not* one who's going to put up with your waiting game."

"It isn't a 'game' to me. It's just how I wanted to be. For me, for the Lord."

"Oh, it's about God, is it? All right, I suppose I can respect that. Still, I don't see how *He* can expect such 'purity' when He made us with as strong of sex drives as we have. Though you clearly like having a man, you seem as if you've got the where-with-all to become a nun, I have to say."

When she said that, something actually clicked. I'd certainly proven well practiced at celibacy; and now that my relationships had taken such a dark and twisted turn, the thought of leaving these two behind to simply serve and seek the Lord sounded refreshing. I wasn't too sure about the 'nun' part however.

I had to give Andrea credit for her honesty, and as such, allowed her to stay the remainder of the night, though apart from me, dismissing her the next morning. I was done with her, and done with James; gracious, I wouldn't really have to deal with confronting him if I didn't want to – Andrea would certainly contend with that the next time she saw him. I was – released.

Chapter 7
Emily

R eady.
    To hunt.

With skill.
With confidence.

Emily was. The summer of seventeen eighty-four was winding into fall, and incredibly, her plan for the 'team hunt' had been accepted by Robert. It hadn't been easy; She'd damn sure needed to prove beyond a shadow of a doubt that she was up to the task. It took a lot of convincing and a solid prospectus to sway her father as to the merits of a full foursome to be out on a group hunt together. But ultimately, he found her logic sound, and was impressed with Emily's initiative.

As per the advice from her mother, Emily had cleverly skewed conversations with Robert on the subject in directions which made it appear as though *he* had come up with the idea. Then, subtle little pushes such as having the slaves participate were her added frostings on the cake. A couple of 'wifely nudges' from Kate here and there were also positive reinforcements to the overall plan. All that was required for success was for Robert to pick hunting treks that were close enough to Chickasaw territory – *and* to be able to find Erika and Jed's village within, most likely, a short window of time. Easy as pie, other than that!

It didn't go 'according to Hoyle' on the first outing by any means. They hadn't traversed nearly close enough to Chickasaw land to even attempt to deviate in that way. But it *did* allow Emily to get a feel for her pairing with Isaiah – even so far as to begin to inform him of her secondary strategy for these hunts. She utilized the same style of cunning with him as with Robert previously; simply outlining the notion, so as not to spook him into thinking about the trouble they could get into if caught.

This, their first haul, was adequate though not stellar in terms of kills. And this was exactly what Emily had hoped for. Successful enough, but leaving plenty of room for the outings to continue. And continue they did.

By the third time, Emily finally got what she wanted – close enough proximity to the Chickasaw areas to at last commence scouting for Erika. As previously planned out with him, she and Isaiah would move out *so* far; then she would move out further still, while he remained stationary, thereby maintaining staggered distances from their break point with Robert and Ben. Perhaps not entirely ideal, but the best she could hope for considering what she had to work with.

In this particular venture, she didn't come away with actually locating her cousin, but she did encounter something *connected* to her – the young wolf. Initially, they saw one another from a distance; and at first Emily was just scared. But she had her gun, and if nothing else, she could return with a righteous kill. Then, something strange

happened. As it was with Erika's own first meeting with it, the wolf neither ran off nor attacked. During this pause, Emily recollected Jed's wife's name, Taynee. She'd found out it meant *born at the return of the moon.* Acting on pure conjecture and a gut instinct, she mused that maybe, just maybe, this could be something of a sign. A wolf howls – at the moon. Some kind of 'spirit animal' sort of thing that might be a form of a – herald? Emily didn't have a lot of time and didn't know when she'd get this kind of chance again. So, she rolled the dice on a very long shot, and moved to approach the wolf.

They were probably within fifteen yards of each other when the wolf stopped its progress and stared at her curiously. Then he turned his snout to the air and reared his head around as if coaxing Emily to go the direction he'd pointed to his rear. He trotted off then, turning about periodically as if checking for if she would give chase. She was nervous, uncertain, but wasn't about to let this go. So, she took off in pursuit of the wolf. They jogged through woods for a while until the tree line ended at a clearing.

There was a lone speck in the far distance of the clearing, and once the wolf saw it, took off at full run towards it. Emily was on the cusp of matching its pace and catch up – to try and see to whom it was running – but heard, at that instant, the distant cry of Isaiah far back behind her. Calling her. She was out of time. All that remained then was for was to stare back for a moment at the distant figure before her, to whom the wolf had gone. She'd never be sure, but she had the strongest feeling she'd found who she'd come for, and swore she would return.

Next time.

As for right now, she turned around and ran at the clip she'd

intended to chase the wolf with – in the opposite direction. Having gained some ground she shouted back, "Isaiah, I'm coming – wait up!" By the time she'd reached him, Ben had already joined him, obviously having been sent to retrieve them both by Robert.

"Come on, missy," Ben began, "time to go. Your father's not happy that you've been gone so long – and so *far* – in *this* direction. He's waitin' for us with our bounty back yonder; didn't want to have to haul it all this way, then backtrack again wit' such a load. So, he jus' sent me ta get ya. What you got to say for yourselves anyway?"

"I was chasing a wolf," said Emily, "but it got a good lead on me and got away. Then I heard Isaiah calling for me and came back straightaway."

"Well," continued Ben, "you's shouldn'ta been split up in the first place, but *you* can explain all 'dat to your pa yourself. You jus' best not get my boy in trouble here, miss. I knows 'dat us in pairs out here be *your* idea."

"You're right, it's *my* plan," she replied, "and I'll see to it Isaiah gets in no trouble from my father, all right? I'll take any and all blame!"

"Good girl," he answered, "now let's go."

· · · ·

Upon their return home, that is exactly what Emily did. She shouldered all the responsibility for having ran off from Isaiah *and* for going into the Indians' land. "Once I'd spotted the wolf, father, I lost track of how far I'd been going. Isaiah even kept up with me, but stopped once he realized how far *in* we'd gone. *Where* we'd gone. He wasn't about cross your wishes to that. So, you see, it's all on me. I'm sorry – especially coming away empty handed without the wolf after crossing the line to go after him."

"And you *should* be, Em," agreed Robert. "Letting the rush of the chase override knowing your position is not the way of the savvy hunter. And in so doing, leaving your partner – also not smart, and bad form. As punishment, I'm charging you with the duties of skinning and packing away all the meat from the hunt, down in the basement – and also *remaining* there the duration of the week. And lest you think Isaiah is innocent in all of this, he is not. Though by rule, not going into the Indian land was correct, *leaving* my daughter while she continued on was worse. But since *you* are taking full responsibility, that is why I'm adding the extended grounding downstairs, for his share of the blame. Am I clear?"

"Crystal," Emily replied, thankful that her partner-in-crime wouldn't reap the consequences of her actions, which were all *her* schemes in the first place, and not on him. Thus, she accepted her punishment, happily even, with no one else receiving Robert's wrath, not to mention the success she perceived she'd had in the search for Erika. Had it been her cousin in the far distance? If so, it appeared she had her own pet wolf now. Or a literal 'spirit animal,' as the Indians might say. One that somehow managed to find *her* – perhaps even sensing that she'd been searching for its master? Possibly. Amazing either way.

Even more amazing was the continued luck Emily was about to have upon completion of her meat packing duties to the ice box. After being served her pittance of dinner from upstairs, she began exploring this cavern of a storehouse she'd been banished to. Having randomly scooted some boxes about, the underlying floor revealed a trap door.

Opening it, she saw a medium sized chest which contained within it – a series of books. Taking out one and opening the cover, Emily discovered it addressed to her mother, saying, *Dearest Kate, May these spells serve and guide you well in the Earthen realm and beyond. Love, Mother.*

No! A spell-book? Of witchcraft? Given by her Grandmother? It couldn't be! Not Mother – *married* to Father – who, if he'd been around a century ago, would probably have hung witches himself! He was nothing if not staunch in his conservative beliefs, not tolerating anything outside of his strict, moral code. Godly, yes, but extreme. Black and white with little wiggle room for acceptance of diversity, be it spiritual, racial or otherwise. No wonder these tomes were buried deep! But, considering the risk if ever found, why even keep them at all? After all, she'd just found them herself!

The unearthing of the grimoires proved fascinating to Emily as she poured through the first volume in the duration of her week-long banishment. This proved to be hardly punishment at all – this was a find! A way to learn more of

Mother in a way she'd ever dreamed – wait! Emily's *dreams* – those she'd had of Erika when she was younger – Kate had encouraged her to confide in her about them. That she could understand, maybe even help interpret, in a way that her father never could – or would! This might be an early indication of Mother's knowledge of *the craft* that she'd missed all those years ago. And now, it was all coming together – coming clear! This was perhaps even *the answer* to Emily's inherent ability to sense her cousin *through* the dreams – of whose existence she'd not even known apart *from* the dreaming!

Then too, there was the inexplicable sense the wolf had *to her*. If the beast *was* in some fashion a 'spirit creature' to Erika, then perhaps it recognized a kind of genetic 'magic' in Emily – *why* it chose to lead her towards its human in the first place.

Much to ponder, and much to learn – from the books, and beyond. If only they weren't so suspect in their content to Robert, she could take one with her upstairs to her room to study; but awfully risky to do. But at the same time, she didn't want to be running down to the basement all the time either, to retrieve one. Nor did she think it wise to be getting herself into trouble all the time with Father so he'd ground her down here again and again. Perhaps she could simply put it in a box and bury it outside someplace; steal away to study when she had the chance, apart from the house itself.

And so it was – Emily returned everything to its place just as she'd found it originally. Upon conclusion of her week's punishment, she'd snuck volume two out with her, later burying it in the adjacent field, all boxed up and secure.

Emily returned to her focus of the hunt and a renewal of their teamed outings – with a little less emphasis on the search for Erika. Her new interest in the grimoires and learning of this craft seemed to temper her feelings of desperation to find her cousin. As hunting seasons and years passed, she continued to look for Erika or her wolf when she was presented the opportunity, but ceased trying to force it as she'd done in the beginning. There was little sense in risking herself or Isaiah to Robert's punishments further. What she *did* do actively as time passed was try out bonding spells towards Erika or the wolf, and locator spells to better find them when she was out their way and had the chance.

Chapter 8
Erika

Erika's introduction of her young wolf to the tribe was a little touch and go in the beginning, but ultimately proved to be quite a boon to the community in the long run. Once she'd shown her mastery over the beast, the people were impressed and everyone came to love *Nashoba* as she'd chosen to call him, meaning Choctaw – wolf.

Nashoba became a great asset as a companion, hunting partner, and perhaps most advantageous of all, an effective liaison between the tribe and any passing wolf packs who might be any threat. In the random occurrences where a traveling pack crossed paths with the village, it was hard to say if Nashoba had ever found *his* original pack, but Erika liked to think so. But the tribe was his pack now, and she was his alpha.

As far as being her hunting partner was concerned, that had proven two-fold in nature as well. There had been *that day*, probably two years past now, when Nashoba had left her for a time, to scout she'd presumed; but upon his return, had lured something or someone back with him. She'd seen a figure in the woods from the clearing where she was, but it had disappeared almost as quickly as she'd spotted it. It was curious and somehow familiar, but she couldn't put her finger on it. And subsequently, she'd picked up on it a number of times since then over the years following. A watcher? A spirit? She couldn't say. But always it came after Nashoba had gone ahead to scout. In some strange way, he seemed to have the connection to draw it out. Perplexing to be sure, but it was never troublesome or cause for worry. Again, it was familiar – comforting in an odd way.

One day, Erika decided to confide in her mother to this phenomenon, to see what Tanyee might have to say about it. As they prepared a meal together, Erika broached the subject. "Ishki," she began, addressing her as mother, "I think Nashoba has 'attached' himself to something – or someone. Every now and then, after running ahead to scout, he'll come back, and someone follows. I think they see and watch me briefly, then disappear. But I sense it's friendly, not a threat..."

"And how long has this been for, my chepota?" asked Tanyee, saying daughter. "Since after the dreams of the other girl stopped, perhaps?"

"Why yes," answered Erika, "perhaps a good while after that. Do you think it's her?"

"It's possible," Tanyee replied. "Let me tell you a little something more about her that you do not know. Her name is Emily and she is the daughter of your father's brother. This man, Robert, has a cold and hardened heart. He cares not for our kind, and holds a strong grudge against Jed for marrying me. He wants his family to have nothing to do with us, and is likely not even aware you exist; if he did, he would think of you as an impure mutt."

"Like a dog? I'm sorry, but that doesn't hurt me, figuring how I feel towards Nashoba."

"Bless you, my chepota, but trust me, coming from him, it is most definitely an insult. An offense to you, to me, and to your Inki. It is why we wish nothing to do with him as well. Now, his wife, Kate and Emily, are another matter. I have only heard this in whispers from Jed, but I believe Kate once told him that before she married Robert, she was something of a 'good witch.' She gave it up because she loved him, and knew he would never tolerate anything of that nature as it is evil to him."

"Does not one such as that use the elements of earth and nature much like we respect the sky, sun, moon and the earth?"

"That is my understanding, yes, dear. And for this reason I suspect that Kate's daughter might also be inherently 'tied' to these things herself. The moon specifically, and how that connects to me – and your wolf. Do you see? Nashoba, as *your* spirit creature, could be sensing the elemental magic that may be within Emily. For whatever reason, whenever she ventures close to our land, she may be drawn to Nashoba's presence, and he in turn, leads her to you. Does this make sense?"

"Kind of. But if this is true, why does she never come closer? Why does she hide and then run away? *This* does not make sense."

"I couldn't say. Perhaps she risks herself in her attempts to see you. Maybe when she is about, she is under Robert's charge and cannot get far enough, nor has time enough for anything more. I'd like to make this better for you if I could – and perhaps I can. I may have an idea."

"That would be wonderful. What is it?"

"Think back to when you knew of each other through your dreams. But then, you got older and they stopped. What if there were a way to

bring them back again? I think I know of such a way. Since we believe that Nashoba could be luring Emily somehow, what if we added a little magic of our own – to him? What if I were to construct a dream-catcher styled collar for him? Wearing it, when he finds Emily, perhaps somehow, he could prompt the opening of the dream-gates once again?"

Erika was mesmerized. What an intriguing idea! Whether it would work or not was impossible to say, but it was something, and it excited the girl greatly. Only time would tell if the endeavor could bring back the dream-walking they once experienced so freely, once again.

• • • •

After a few short weeks, there came the day when Erika took a special moment to present Nashoba with his new, and hopefully-magical, collar. Tanyee's craftsmanship was exquisite; the tassels very short so as not to interfere with the wolf's movements, the feathers robust and durable, to be able to take the wear and tear he would no doubt apply.

They were out in the woods scouting with Jed when she took Nashoba aside and knelt down to show him the collar. She playfully rustled the coat of his neck before putting it on. Once adjusted, she stepped back, admiring how it looked on him. The thickness of the feathers made it appear as though he had a lion's mane – a good look for him. 'Fashion' aside, the important thing was for this to work; for the purpose of what a dreamcatcher was to spark whatever magic might be in Emily when Nashoba next encountered her – and bring back the dreams.

• • • •

Chapter 9

Charissa

L ondon, 1788 – Continuing at the university the next few years with both James and Andrea still present didn't prove easy. But, I threw myself into my studies, and back more whole-heartedly to the Lord. I think doing so allowed me to remain in my education there, and not be too distracted by their presence and the reminder of the heartbreak. By the time of my completion, the two had since graduated, so I was able to round out my last years there mostly healed, being entirely free of them presently.

My parents were disappointed to the squandered potential of an expected marriage, which they gave me endless grief about. Though I'd been explicit as to the details of how things had gone awry, they seemed convinced that, somehow, I'd not handled it intelligently. That perhaps, I should've compromised myself for the sake of achieving that all-important state of matrimony. Hogwash!

However, on the other side of that coin, they *did* take solace that at least that which they'd invested in my education would be put to use. It was definitely looking like I'd have to make my own way!

One core residual *had* remained from the experience though. From the epiphany I'd had in my final hours with Andrea – the idea of the refreshment of spirit in leaving them and serving God. I took that mindset with me as I endeavored after college to seek out the ministry to that end vocationally.

– A Year Later –

I stared out across the river Thames as I often did after a good day's work of serving God in his house, the Church of England, London. I would come here to ponder and pray, thankful for the blessing of my station, a *female* with aspirations toward the Anglican priesthood. As a solitary woman with a bent to do Christ the Lord's work, I diligently sought any role I might fill, short of becoming a nun, making every effort necessary that they might have me. As still a relatively young lady, *that* level of commitment was not quite as far as I wanted to go.

I mused that I might still entertain the companionship of a man again at some point. The stain of James, Andrea and the turmoil life had become because of them, had me in the place where I wasn't ready for another man just yet. Still, the Fathers – who they were as men and servants – gave me hope. I worked with them, shared with them, got to know them through our duties together. And *if this* was what a man could truly be, then I might be very premature to commit to the sisterhood, vowing celibacy from the opposite sex, as the men I admired *had*. For the present, my spirit was free, to be myself in serving God, and simply explore what my life could be, in all of its many choices. Not to mention the time I needed to truly get on my feet.

But I'm getting ahead of myself. It took a lot of perseverance and persistence to even become accepted before being around the priests at all. I will confess that my family's standing and being a supporter of the church didn't hurt my case. It began simply, merely leading prayer and caring for those in need, or looking after children. What I had my eyes on though, were some of the upcoming missionary trips in the planning stages within the next few years. To venture out from home and the familiar while spreading the good news felt like where God was leading me. To spread the word to peoples who knew nothing of it sounded glorious. To experience cultures vastly different and explore parts of the world I might never see otherwise seemed entirely enriching. I knew it would be rigorous and at times difficult, but I didn't care. I would have though, if I had eyes that could see the future.

My favorite spot to go to contemplate was upon the London Bridge overlooking the Thames. Well, my second favorite anyway. The absolute best site was miles east where the river broadens towards the North Sea; Canvey Island across from Alhallows and the Isle of Grain. This is where the waterway can really draw you in and take you away. But it didn't need to this day; to quell my spirit and rest my soul was all that was necessary, so London Bridge served just fine.

Night was falling and a brilliant full moon was coming up in the sky. As I took it in, my mind went to one of the aforementioned places – *Alhallows* – which, combined with the moon, made me giggle to think of witches and werewolves. Again, if I could've only known the future – I might not have laughed. Then again, I *may* have...

• • • •

Chapter 10

Emily

It was another spring day promising the spoils of a good hunt. The venture of the four hunters had become more than stockpiling game for the winter by this time. It was now something they'd all come to thoroughly enjoy doing together, regardless of the time of year. Anytime was a good time, provided the game was plentiful, as long as it wasn't too hot or cold. This pleased Emily no end, and her continued patience in waiting it out for the moments to seek out her cousin or her wolf had certainly paid off. This day was no exception as once more, their course took them closer to the Chickasaw lands.

Emily and Isaiah had gone off to their respective route in that direction, and Em moved out into the territory on her own to see what the day might bring. Before long, yet another encounter with Nashoba was to be had. When she saw him and approached, she marveled asking, "What is this?" observing the new collar. "This is beautiful, boy," she said, kneeling down to him to see closer. "If I didn't know better, I'd say this looks like a – dreamcatcher. But it's a collar at the same time. That's different," she mused, curious. As she explored the accessory with her fingers, then moved her hand to pet him, she caught his eyes, and he, hers.

Now by this time, Emily had become more practiced from her reading and study of the grimoires, having advanced to higher proficiency in her abilities to use – *and detect* – magic. And she sensed it here, plainly. While looking into Nashoba's eyes, she felt herself slipping into a daydream. It was pleasant, seeing images of both herself *and* Erika in the woods hunting. They weren't together, but in their respective places; herself with Robert and their slaves, Erika with Jed, Nashoba and other tribesmen. And lastly, she saw an image of a bow and a rifle crisscrossed against each other on the ground, perhaps meaning that the girls' two forms of hunting would one day intersect? Then she snapped out of it.

"Oh my," she gasped, reeling. Looking at him and scuffing his fur, she asked, "Did *you* do that? Somebody took the time to make this – and to send you out with it on. Somebody who knows – that you know how to find *me*. Because I feel like this is *for* me. And for *her.* Thank you," she said, hugging him. "I better go, not follow you today. My time's running short, as usual. But, from *that,* I feel like I got what I came for already. Thanks, wolf," she finished, and turned to go.

• • • •

That night, and on many nights to follow, Emily's dreamworld again opened up to Erika's. It wasn't quite the same as how they were entirely lucid with each other when they were children, but it was surely *something.* Whatever happened during that daydream moment with Nashoba had definitely flipped a switch.

Emily saw Erika again in settings like with her father, mother, wolf, and others of the tribe. Her favorites were with Jed and the wolf. Especially the wolf. For she actually *knew* him in real life, had a connection, and swore she would one day with her cousin and her uncle too.

One day, Emily awoke as she often did when having dreamt of her uncle – saddened. Sad because of fond yet vague memories of him, and not being able to see him for most of her life. Because of who he married, the Native woman that her father, his brother, despised. She who he'll have no part of. And now, by lineage, the daughter to whom Emily couldn't see, except for in her covert operations into their land, and her 'secret agent contact' thereto, the wolf.

Very nearly thirteen years old now, and the rebellious nature of teen-hood beginning to set in, she thought, *enough.* She should finally go to her father, stand up and say, 'no more.' Perhaps even this very day. And to that effect, she began to pick up on the scent of cooking eggs and bacon floating down the hall to her room; that which would herald family time around the table, a perfect opportunity to confront her father, should she choose to do so.

Almost as if on-cue, Kate called out from the kitchen loud enough to be heard from Emily's room. "Breakfast is ready, darling. Time to come join us!"

"Be right there, Mother," Emily answered, debating with herself. Just another typical family mealtime, or a day of reckoning with Father? She arrived to the breakfast table hesitant, uncertain. A maid served their courses, grace was said, and everyone proceeded to dig in. Robert and Kate chit-chatted while Emily remained quiet. Her extended

silence at last drew attention from her father.

"You're awfully quiet this morning, Emily. Nothing to add to the conversation, dear?" he asked as if expectant for her participation. That was pretty much all it took.

"Yes I *do,* father," she replied coldly. "I'd like to share about the dream I had of Uncle Jed last night. You remember your brother, Jed, yes? I do, but only barely. Because you've kept him from me – practically my whole life!" She was almost shouting now. "Did you know he has a daughter now, Father?"

Kate held back a gasp, covering up her mouth, fearful of what Emily might say next, what it could reveal. To her relief, Em's following words *did not* betray anything of the magic that could risk them both. What she espoused put only herself in the way of Robert's wrath; and he glared at her intensely.

"I've seen her, Father," continued Emily, "in the lands where I'm not allowed – but I go to anyway, when I get the chance. I've seen her with Jed – an Indian girl a little younger than me. I've seen by the way they interact that she's his. But I only ever have time to see them briefly. I've always got to get back in time so Isaiah and I aren't caught. But I can't take it anymore, Father. I'm tired of sneaking out to do it, and I'm *sick* of not being able to see the rest of my family!"

"Well, you needn't worry any longer about sneaking off on the hunts to go look for them!" he raged, rising from his seat. "As of this moment, you are *never* to go hunting with me – *ever again!* I cannot believe I'm hearing this – I presumed this behavior was quelled long ago when you were first caught in the act and punished to the basement! But apparently, I have been duped, by my own daughter,

for God only knows how long! *Why* I've chosen to distance myself, and thereby my family as a whole, from my brother are my own reasons – which will *not* be questioned! Least of all by you, young lady!"

"I do not question your *reasons,* Father," she replied simply. "I don't care what they are. I just question – *you!*"

"Why you ungrateful little witch! How dare you?" roared Robert, moving swiftly toward Emily with hand raised. He connected with her face knocking her from her chair to the floor. Towering over her and about to deliver yet another blow, Kate intervened, intercepting his next swing.

"Stop it, Robert!" she screamed, holding him away from Emily. "Clearly, she's disrespecting and goading you, but enough! Step away please, love."

Getting a hold of himself, Robert acquiesced, but not before giving Emily a final piece of his mind. *"You* – finish your breakfast, then do your chores – after which you're grounded to the basement again – for a duration I've yet to decide!" He then turned from his wife and daughter and stormed off.

In his wake, Kate helped Emily up from the floor and held her, weeping. "What in God's name prompted all of that?" she sobbed to Em, still holding her. "You dreamt of Jed, you said? Are you dreaming of his daughter again too?"

"Yes..." she replied to the last two questions. With respect to the first, she said, "This last dream just made me so sad. Sad that I can't see my uncle, or my cousin, or even my aunt! And it's never going to change! You said *I* goaded Father just now. But *he* goaded me when he pushed for me to talk, like I'm 'supposed' to. I was already thinking

about standing up to him when I woke up, but I held back when I came in to eat. But then he had to insist, so I told him what was on my mind."

"I appreciate that you said nothing of knowing about the girl *through* the dreams," Kate responded, "but to take the responsibility for so many consequences, not to mention the punishment you're going to get – it's too much, my love! And now you'll be losing the one opportunity to see her that you've worked so long and hard to maintain.

Not if I go out there all on my own and just disregard his rules, Emily thought to herself. *And damn the consequences.*

Chapter 11
Em – Erika

After her scolding and immediate directive to completion of her chores around the cabin, Emily trudged through her work dutifully yet distractedly. As lunchtime approached and her tasks all but done, she found she had no appetite for a meal, much less more exposure to her father's presence. The basement didn't matter; there were still more grimoires to read. Instead, she opted to bolt, taking off for the woods in answer to the call to clear her mind in the forest's beauty.

Deeper and deeper into the woodland she ventured, until she was so far removed that she'd unwittingly stumbled once more into Chickasaw Territory. Or *seemingly* without conscious thought. Perhaps because she'd been so heated in her argument with her father regarding her uncle's chosen family, she'd naturally navigated here on instinct. After all, she'd been coming here for years to peek in upon the extended family whom she was not allowed to know.

Emily didn't know a lot about the Indian culture but she was learning. She knew they believed in earth and air and animal spirits. And as she walked and breathed and listened, she felt it – took it all in. As she did so, she heard the creatures around go silent, and the hush of one in particular, sensing it had become quarry to another. Another who was not – *another* creature.

Emily crouched down into the brush to see that the hunter wasn't a man either – but a girl, about her own age; the one she knew to be Erika. The girl moved with finesse and stealth, steadily tracking a deer in the distance. The doe moved and paused; then paused and moved again, trying to sense the best moment for a full retreat. It would be in *that* moment when her cousin's bow would launch its arrow for the killing strike.

The shaft's deadly point found home and felled the deer into a heap. The shot was true, but the animal's death-knell not immediate. In response, Erika ran to her prey, not wanting it's suffering to linger. She removed her blade from her hip, gently yet firmly slicing the deer's throat to expedite its spirit's departure. Then she cradled its head in one arm while placing her palm to its forehead. She closed her eyes beginning to softly croon while gently rocking the beast from side to side.

Though she'd secretly spied on her often, Emily had never seen her hunt much before, and was taken by her cousin's behavior post-kill, openly sniffling at her touching actions. Emily's sounds alerted the other girl to her presence in hiding.

The she-hunter whirled around, still cradling the dear, demanding, "Who's there? Man or beast, show yourself!"

Erika was clearly talking in her native tongue, but Emily understood her perfectly well. As she moved out from the bushes holding her hands in truce, she wondered about that. She knew she'd heard words that were not English, but still knew exactly what the young huntress had asked. The Holy Spirit's gift of interpreting foreign tongues perhaps?

"I'm sorry," said Emily, suddenly embarrassed for spying. Not that she hadn't done so a hundred times before. "I was just wandering the forest and – I guess I'd gone further than I'd thought. I didn't mean to invade your hunting ground."

The other girl assessed Emily's demeanor and candor with a look of scrutiny. Finally, she nodded in acceptance and waved for Emily to put her hands down. She felt oddly at ease with this stranger – as though she *were not* one. "It is all right," she began, now speaking in clear English, noting Emily as a colonial. "I believe you – though you're right, you've wandered a long way. My name is Erika, and it is good to finally meet you. I'm fairly sure you are – Emily."

"That's me," answered Em, approaching Erika to formally greet her. *"Your name* – not exactly Chickasaw is it?"

"No, it's not," replied the native girl, "My father picked it, and he's not Indian."

"I've hunted a lot with my father before," *and been hunting you,* Emily thought to herself as she continued, "but though I'm good with a gun – I'm not quite the hunter you are."

"I hope my kill did not scare you," Erika responded apologetically. "I do not think of it as such – as 'killing,' that is. Yes, I've taken this animal's life, but it is to the sustenance of my tribe, and I thank it for its sacrifice."

"Yes, Erika, I saw *that*," Emily replied. "It intrigued and touched me, the way you attended to the deer after you got it. I've never seen such a thing before. It made me almost cry."

"And that's what gave you away, girl," said Erika. "It is not the white man's way to take life or land and be grateful for it. He believes it is his dominion to do so, thus knows little of 'life's circle.' I am thankful that my father, also a white man, is *not* of that way."

Emily was in the middle of musing over Erika's former words as she realized the impact of her latter ones. "Your *white dad!*" Emily exclaimed, realizing her opening to say who they were to one another had presented itself. "Erika," Emily began, "Do you know that your father has a brother – one who doesn't see him – because of *his* prejudice against your people?"

Erika looked at her with clarity – as though the floodgates had opened from Emily's question. "I know he *does* – and I know he's *your* father! My mother told me everything when I was old enough to make sense of it. Though I have to admit, I still *cannot* make sense of why your Inki is the way he is."

Suddenly, all that led to Emily's being here in this moment came crashing upon her. The argument with her Dad over his brother and his native woman that Robert simply wouldn't tolerate. Emily's drive for years to connect with family she was not allowed to see because of Robert's bigotry. Stewing over it throughout her chores, and fleeing here to these woods to escape it all – finally face-to-face with her cousin with the chance to be transparent! She turned from Erika, gasping a deep breath of emotion, overwhelmed suddenly, at the flood of everything welling up within her.

Erika gave her space as she could see her grappling with something – but not for long. *"Emily!"* she cried finally, laying her hand upon the other girl's shoulder, turning her around. "I can see that you're struggling with whatever it is you're trying to say – but *what* are you trying to say?

"It's my father – and I hate him!" Emily shouted. Upon her outburst of this announcement, she collapsed into Erika, crying and thumping her fists into the Chickasaw girl in frustration.

Not really knowing what else to do between this improbable statement *and* Emily's emotional behavior, Erika simply accepted the embrace, albeit a ferocious one. As she held her, the pounding subsided, fists turned to open hands that held the one they'd longed to for so long.

Suddenly, as the hug netted its result, Erika backed up, starring Emily straight in the face. "It's you at last!" she pronounced. "The one I used to dream of, and now do again. The one who's presence I've sensed watching me from a distance in the woods many times! Why? Why so long of watching and dreaming? Why haven't you come to me like this before, Emily?"

"Because I'm a coward! I do what I'm told because I've been scared of the consequences – because I'm afraid of my father! If I just came out here and watched, then I wasn't guilty of disobeying him – I *never* actually interacted with you."

"But not today," said Erika.

"No, *today* was too much. We had a huge fight, and I couldn't take it anymore. I came out here like I have before, but *now* I'm talking to you."

"Though you were still in hiding till I became aware of you. Would you have come out if I hadn't heard you?"

"Yes, I would've! Because today I decided I wasn't going to put up with it any longer! And now it's happened, and here we are."

"Yes, finally. Tell me more of how we dream of one another? How do *you* think it happens?"

"I'm not sure, but I think it probably has to do with my mother. She used to be a witch before she met my father, I found out. She gave it up, but perhaps it's passed onto me. My longing to see you and your dad for so long worked into dreaming powers perhaps?

"That's what my Ishki thought. I remember seeing you in my dreams a lot – when we were little kids – but then we got older, and they stopped. As I think about it, *that's* when I started sensing eyes upon me in the woods when I was hunting. But I never saw you for long when I looked. But it was always *you*."

"Yes, when the dreams started going away, I got this pull to wander and actually look for you. I couldn't help myself."

"But now, the dreams are back because of the dream-catcher collar Mother put on my wolf, and *that* opened us up again."

"I guess so. He's always helped me find you. And however he helped to bring the dreams back with the catcher, it made me realize how mad I've been over being apart from you and Jed all this time. Up until today and my spilling the beans about you in my anger, Father didn't even know you existed!"

Erika's face went sad in disbelief. Not only was this entire disclosure hard to process, but such overwhelming bigotry made her heart sick. It wasn't that she was ignorant of the tensions between Americans and Natives, nor even their fathers, but to have it hit so close to home, being the very core of an inability to see a relative, hurt. "I'm just

glad," she began, still recovering, "that you're here at last, talking to me. But what is it going to cost you when you return? Won't it be even harder to come back again?"

"Of course it will. Next to impossible. I can't even guess how long I'll be punished for. He's already told me I can't go hunting with him anymore. And I'll probably be locked in the basement for months when he finds out I ran off out here."

"Then I will come to you. I have nothing of the same rules holding me back as you do. I cannot imagine having met you at last, only to not see you again for more years to come."

"How will you find me?" asked Emily, knowing Erika didn't know where she lived.

"With Nashoba, naturally! He's allowed *you* to find me so many times – he'll be able to do the same in *my* search for you."

"That's his name, 'Nashoba'? I like that, it's beautiful. It's nice to know what he's called too."

"Thank you. It means, Chactow – wolf. I named him myself, and Ishki made the 'catcher-collar' to help him better connect with you – and the magic she guesses you've inherited from your Ishki."

"It worked. He sensed my magic, and re-opened our dreaming of each other again. I've been practicing more, learning spells from my mother's old books I found the first time I was punished when caught going into your land. They were in the basement where he puts me when I've been 'bad.'"

"That's horrible."

"I don't care anymore. When I go home and am thrown back down there, it'll give me more time to study the rest of the books, and get

really good at this. Just like I did with hunting."

"Be careful, please."

"I will, don't worry. And wait for me to dream to you to tell you when it's safe to come. There's no sense in your coming when I'm grounded below and can't really get out."

Thus having devised a relative plan for their future encounters, Erika walked and talked with Emily part of the way back as she returned to Clarksville and the slew of Robert's punishments awaiting her there.

Chapter 12
Charissa

he Caribbean, 1790 – The island looked peaceful and beautiful enough when we approached it; why wouldn't it when you've sailed the Caribbean and come to an isle such as St. Vincent? But when you're on a missionary journey to reach out to a native tribe in hopes of conversion, you never *truly* know what you're getting into, no matter how idyllic it looks at the beginning, nor how sure you are in your faith.

As far as we knew, we were simply representing the Holy Catholic Church of England, to share Christ Jesus with the indigenous peoples. We trekked from the shores on inland, searching for signs of habitation. We found it slowly, frightfully – when jungle sounds came to us from this way and that. Animals? Tribesmen? We couldn't know until they were upon us – surrounding us. Taking us. We spoke out – cried out to them of Jesus's love and peace to all men. Oh, if only the Holy Ghost had come and opened their ears to our tongue – and ours to theirs. But she did not come, not this day.

Some of us, though not antagonistic, *did* attempt some defense against our impending capture. Those who doing so paid the price in being beaten and were unconscious by the time we reached their village. Those, such as myself who did not, were simply led away by force by these clansmen.

They were ghastly, faces painted with a white, chalky substance, encircling their eyes and mouths. It was like blackface, eerie and disturbing. Their camp was equally frightening; I saw a pot with a duck's flesh, goose flesh – and a man's. There was likewise the head of a young man fastened to a post, yet *bleeding,* and drinking vessels made of skulls. I noted also the bones of men's arms and legs on the heads of their arrows. The reports of Columbus' travels in this area were starting to dawn on me as to just what kind of natives it appeared we'd been sent to reach. Natives with whom you do not survive the encounter.

I *did* – but only I alone. And only after being prodded and poked to reveal that I was undefiled by man, by James. As such, I was a delicacy – one I would be preserved for to *drink* – not eat. Not – as the rest of my companions were.

Over time, my spirit was beaten and broken; my blood drained – and drunk. I said I'd lived – but only after a fashion. I was un-dead – in *their* sins.

So, my mission trip to the West Indies had brought us unwittingly into this tribe of cannibals; and they'd used me to drink from for months on end. But that alone wasn't *entirely* what turned me. As I've said, I was the 'fine wine' for the tribes' family meal each week. There came a point when there was some special celebration that lasted over the course of several days; like an extended holiday we might observe in our civilized countries. During that period, they'd drained me

utterly. They'd gotten careless – and I believe I literally *died.*

When they'd realized what they'd done, draining their precious virgin 'drink' to death, they weren't having it. They'd sought out a medicine-man, witch-doctor, whatever you want to call him, from a neighboring tribe; as they did not have one of their own. It wasn't a clan they were on the best of terms with; it was akin to relations between Scotland and England prior to the union of a 'United Kingdom.' The other tribe had their own reasons for offering the 'aid,' as I'd find out later.

Now, this shaman came in, performed magics upon me, and I believe, gave me his own blood in order to somehow, revive my essence. I *felt* it; his breath on me, my teeth in his wrist taking in *his* blood – the tiny bit *I* had left comingling with his, all of it funneling together, recreating me as a monster like himself.

It worked obviously, and I clearly wasn't the same. I'd become as he was – some kind of cannibal-vampire hybrid. And once the change occurred, it was clear why he'd done it for them. Not to help them, but to destroy them. Once I'd transformed into this unholy thing, I went on a rampage throughout the village, killing and drinking everyone I could.

My months of bondage to them, the slaughter and consumption of *my* people – it all came out in a murderous rage that wouldn't stop until I'd slain all of them who didn't get away.

Once that was all over, I'd decided I was going to go back to England and seek vengeance upon those who'd sent us, no matter how long it took me. *Not* the fathers whom I'd admired, but the cardinals and the bishops above them; those who'd planned out the missions' journey years in advance. The one I'd anxiously waited for – like an ignorant sheep to slaughter.

Perhaps I'd even seek out James and Andrea as well, just for good measure. A 'special thanks' to him as it were. Had he been successful in 'making me a woman,' I'd be dead, consumed as food like the rest of my missionary companions. If they were still together, perhaps I could 'thank' them both, together.

And so it went – I'd set my mind to exact my revenge. Ultimately, it took me a couple of years to return to England from where I'd been stranded on the isle. But return I did, by land and by sea, steadfastly laying out my dastardly plans to pick off those miserable bishops one by bloody one.

It was interesting to watch my evolution as a predator. I'd begun as a rampant animal on the island; simply attacking and killing anyone before me, for there was no distinction. They were *all* guilty, evil. Now, in seeking out these 'civilized' church fathers, I'd become calculated and cunning, *patiently* steering towards my murderous goals. The girl who was but a few short years ago, concerned only with learning and friendships seemed long gone. A blissful, ignorant little child – whom these 'men of the cloth' had dashed away by sending her and others to a lions' den – for what? Advancement of territories? England's reign to extend elsewhere? One obligatory 'humanitarian effort' to convert a people prior to their removal or extermination? I was now the only 'un-living' result of that endeavor which *had* to be someone's decision to proceed with. An endeavor that was probably all but forgotten by now. But I would remind them – oh, how I would.

Chapter 13

Erika

Erika sat with her Father and Mother following the evening meal, telling them of her monumental meeting with her cousin that day. Jed had already known as he'd been her chaperon during the time it happened; though he'd gone off in another direction with Nashoba when the girls met. Erika had felt bad for not taking Emily back to greet Jed, but had been more worried about getting Em on her way in hopes of lessening the trouble she was already in.

"She'd had a big fight with her father earlier in the day," Erika explained, "and simply followed her instincts to come to the woods – to come to us. Not like before on her hunting trips stealing away to look for me; *just like* you'd guessed, Ishki," she continued, acknowledging Tanyee's hunch from a while back. "She was rash to do it, but very brave in her resolve to no longer obey Robert's silly rules for her."

"Or very stupid," offered Jed. "Robert's going to be awfully hard on her for running off like she did. If she's smart, she'll say nothing of meeting you; just went off somewhere – *anywhere* but here."

"I'd like to think so," replied his daughter, "but I'm not sure. She was very angry with him, and didn't seem to care how badly she's punished. I sort of feel like it's *our* fault in a way – for sending out Nashoba with the dream collar – because it definitely worked. And if she weren't dreaming of us again, she might have continued to keep herself in check. But now..."

Tanyee chimed in and said, "You are right, chepota, to take some responsibility; but honestly, with the persistence you *both* have maintained to one another over the years, this was bound to happen eventually."

"I am shamed to say," Erika replied, "that she has made far more effort to it than I. I realize now that she has always overcome more obstacles and taken much risk to look for me, while I've done neither." As she made the pronouncement, she looked at them both squarely. "I ask you both now for your permission to take my proper turn in seeking *her* out, as she has me. She suspects she shall be grounded in her basement for some time. She says she will try to dream to me when the time comes that she's no longer banished. I told her that I would come to her henceforth as I have none of the same rules that she does, keeping us apart. Will you allow me?"

Tanyee was quick to say, "Of course you may, absolutely!"

Jed raised his hand in pause to this, and said, *"Only so long* as you're *very* careful and never go too close to their land or their home. I *know* my brother and I'm quite sure he'd be a danger to you. You understand?"

"Yes, Inki, I almost wish I didn't, but I *do* – and I *will* – be careful. But it will probably be a while until I go..."

"Whenever the time comes, see that you are," concluded Jed.

. . . .

Nights later, Erika walked under the full moon light with Nashoba, strolling together through the nearby woods. The wolf whined at her, restless to her paradoxical mood. She was simultaneously as elated and saddened as she'd ever been. Joyous to at last meet her beloved cousin, and sorrowful to the abuses she knew Emily would be enduring. Not to mention furious with herself for not making the same attempts to reach out as Em had.

Suddenly, Nashoba howled out, baying at the moon, and snapping Erika out of her emotional dilemma. Startled, she turned her attention to him and knelt down to his side, howling along with him. It allowed for her to let all these feelings out in sustained cries. She looked to her pet and wondered if it was the same for him. In that one moment, bellowing out together, she almost felt like she knew what it was to *be* the wolf. Yes, he was indeed her 'spirit animal,' but this felt as though it was moving further beyond that.

She knew of the legend of the lycanthrope, man *into* beast under the moon – but this was magic surpassing even that of her culture's beliefs. It suddenly struck her that she now knew someone practicing such magics, and thought to herself – *hmmn*. Food for thought – for later, as Nashoba had her attention again – with something else. He was craning his neck downward quirkily, as though he wanted the dream collar *off*. No sooner had she removed it, he began nudging it at her, hard, as if he wanted *her* to take it, do something with it.

"What, boy? What are you after? Do you want *me* – to wear it?" she questioned.

He howled.

"Yes?"

He howled again.

"All right," she agreed, putting it around her neck. She knelt back down to face him, trying further to figure this out. "Now what?"

He grumbled as if she was on the right track. He caught her eyes, just as he had Emily's that day she'd first seen him with the new collar. All at once, she was his. As before with Em, Erika felt herself falling into the place of daydream, seeing images of Emily in her basement with her books. She was reciting something, a spell no doubt. Next, she saw her ascend the stairs, wave a hand unlocking the door, advancing through the house, and *passing right by her father*, completely unnoticed. She'd passed slaves and servants, but they too seemed oblivious to her presence. Only one, probably her mother, appeared to have any sense that someone was afoot; but here too, she didn't visibly *see* Em as she exited the house.

Now, Erika viewed Emily as though she were approaching her. As she grew closer, she spoke, *Come to me when you can. It is safe, they cannot see me – see us. My punishment no longer holds me.*

With that, Erika snapped out of the vision. Emily had dreamt to her – while awake even! She still had a clear connection to Nashoba and the collar, for the wolf had followed commands perfectly, giving Erika that which she needed to open the dream gate and receive the message! And what was that Em had used to leave her dungeon – some kind of 'cloaking spell'? Flawless! It appeared that Emily's resolve knew no bounds. Henceforth, Erika's would not either.

· · · ·

Chapter 14
Charissa

ondon, 1793 – If *The Times* had invented the use of spot color to the paper yet, I'd have been helping them add *a lot* of red – blood red. For, by this time I'd been adding much ink to their rag from the trail of bishop blood I'd been leaving. It was scandalous. I made it a point to leave my calling card; a wine goblet with blood residue plus a small, partially bitten, blood-stained bread loaf next to the bodies of my victims – for the irony.

Did I say victims? No, I meant *sacrifices*. **Justice** for how we'd been sacrificed *by them*. I'd been careful and precise to research those whom were responsible for the 'missionary trip' we'd been sent on, so that I'd not be spilling innocent blood, as ours had been. As I've said, I'd admired the priests. Still did, though I must admit, not as much as before. As such, I wasn't going to murder anyone who didn't have it coming. You see? I *was* evolving as my darker self – not just the killing machine I'd been at the start – now I bit with 'fangs of righteousness.' At least that's what I told myself.

All told, there were at least half a dozen men who'd partaken in the conception and planning of the mission. I'd saved the 'top of the food chain' for last, an arch-bishop who I'd found had brokered politically as well in the bloody little scheme. The worst for last – *only fitting* I thought. In between the 'holy' men, I'd sprinkled confusion for the authorities by adding James here, and Andrea there; so as to mix up the general pattern I'd established, befuddling the police and press no end. Andrea had been a special treat to me, as I'd actually decided to *turn,* and not just murder her. Her character was different from the norm, one whom I felt would embrace, far better than even I, this beastly existence. My gift to her for her friendship. Truly.

The trouble with this 'blood bath' I'd immersed myself into was this: it was addictive. As with anything, the more you do it, the more you have a taste for it. And with all the attention I'd garnered in my murder-scene displays, it had begun to close in on me. Though I'd received much gratification in confounding the investigators, they weren't entirely stupid. Over the course of the many months I'd been at it, an inspector or two actually came my direction asking questions – it appeared I'd become a 'person of interest.'

Once again, this time by my own hand, I was going to have to depart England and cross the sea. I'd no interest in that of missions anymore, nor serving the Church, whom I no longer recognized, really, as 'the Lord's.' Now, I mused, I would go where everyone was going these days – to 'the land of opportunity' – to America.

• • • •

Chapter 15
Em - Erika

It had been invigorating, pure release literally, to have cast an effective cloaking spell and just waltz her way out of the basement, through the house and straight outside without anyone noticing her. Pure perfection, except for the hesitancy Emily had picked up from her Mom, likely sensing, though not seeing her visibly. That was explainable as Kate still possessed her magic, however rusty it might be.

Standing outdoors near the field she'd buried the grimoires she'd already read, she felt as accomplished as she ever had hunting with Robert. Not that those weren't once fond memories, but considering how he treated her these days, these new recollections definitely trumped the old. Plus, the fact of having learned this spell efficiently, she now had a permanent leg-up on him. A far better position to be in, no question. She wondered to herself if the simultaneous sharing of those events into the dream landscape unto Erika had been equally as efficient? Nearly impossible to be sure at this juncture. Only the nighttime would tell, when she slept and Erika could dream back to say if she'd received or not.

• • • •

Dream-walking was not an exact science, so it took a few nights before Emily had any confirmation whether her cousin had 'gotten the message.' One morning a few days later, Emily awoke in her basement, pleased with the dream she'd had that night. She *had* dreamt of Erika, and it was made known that the vision of her leaving her dungeon had indeed been received. Erika had said that she would try to come to Emily by the next day. Excellent. She would be ready.

When tomorrow had come, Kate stood at the kitchen window whispering a quiet "be careful, Em," into the empty air as she sensed the exit of her unseen daughter out the back door.

A few miles out, Erika trudged across a field with Nashoba at her side; he ever the scout to lead his master to her target. As the dot in the distance she'd guessed was Emily's house grew closer, the thin air before her shimmered, slowly revealing what looked like a ghost materializing from the other side. *Emily* – lifting the spell and 'decloaking' before her very eyes. Emily grinned at her confidently as if knowing she'd just made as grand an entrance as one could possibly make.

Smiling back, Erika spread her arms out wide to receive her cousin's embrace. As they held each other, Nashoba got up on his hind legs, bouncing about; he wanting equal share of attention in the tender moment.

Emily cuddled in close to him, giving him the affection he sought. "Gooood booyy," she crooned, jiggling his dream collar. "You did sooo good, giving this to your master so she could 'see!' Good boy!"

"Yes," Erika began, "that was a strange moment. I didn't know what he was up to at first with all of that. But once I took his cues and put it on, it all came clear. I have to say, Em, with what you've done using the collar and this cloaking spell you're doing, you seem to be getting very good at this 'witchery.'"

"'Witchery,' you say? I like the sound of that! I guess I'm getting the hang of it. Everything I'm doing seems to be working pretty well. And it *is* getting me out of the basement early!"

"How much longer are you supposedly grounded for?" asked Erika.

"I don't know, probably another month or so. Less if Mom has her way. She thinks it's cruel."

"It *is*."

"Of course it is. But it doesn't really matter to me anymore; I'm obviously not *truly* bound by it now. Besides, I'm learning 'witchery' with all of Mom's books down there. Basically, I'm turning his punishments to my advantage."

"Don't get overconfident. He's still your father – and that could make things dangerous."

"I'll bet *your* father told you that – that mine could be a danger – to *you*."

"He *did* say that, how did you know? Speaking of Inki, he accompanied me today, but stayed back to give us some privacy. I felt bad that we didn't take the time before – would you like to go and see him now?"

"I would love nothing more, cousin. Please, let's go!"

A short time later, the girls approached Jed from a distance as Nashoba quickly closed the gap, dashing to greet him exuberantly. Moments later, uncle and niece lovingly embraced, trying to melt away the decade-long span since they'd last seen each other.

"My God, you've grown, Em!" Jed exclaimed, easing her back to take a good look. "You're a young lady now! Damn Robert for keeping us apart all this time!"

"Yes, he's a fool, I know," agreed Emily. "But it doesn't matter any longer, I'm done with his foolishness – I'm *here* now at last – with you, with her."

"Because you're learning 'the craft,' right Em?" pressed Jed. "Be wise, niece. Though you're feeling your oats now with the powers you're learning, don't underestimate my brother. If you think he's been bad about me with Indians, *imagine* how he'll be about witchcraft if he finds out. His attitudes won't be far removed from the witch hunters of a hundred years ago in Salem. Think of your mother if not yourself."

"Don't worry, Uncle Jed, I am mindful. I'll be careful and not misuse what I'm learning. Mother made a choice to stop, and I must respect that, and her reasons for doing so. Even if I don't respect – him."

"You *should* still respect him *because* he's your father, Em. It's what the good book says."

"Well, at least *you* don't misuse the Bible the way he does, Uncle Jed. All right, I'll try."

"Good! Speaking of that, we should let you get back. You don't want to be gone too long, lest you be found out, and more trouble ensues," Jed concluded.

With that, Erika led Emily on her way back towards home, while Nashoba remained behind with Jed.

"Before you go, Em, there's something I want to ask you about, if you don't mind," said Erika.

"Of course not, anything, cousin."

"Well, you have this close connection with Nashoba, just as I do. And he's my 'spirit-dog,' you know. Something happened the same night he had me wear the collar and you showed me what you were able to do. It was just before that. I'd been upset with myself over not making a better effort to seek you out as you had me all this time. Anyway, he shook me out of it by howling at the moon. Then I joined him, and we howled out together. In that moment, I actually felt 'wolf-like.' It was as bonded to him as I'd ever felt. It was magic. And now I know that *you're* magic. So, I was wondering..."

"...If *I* could use my magic, through my already-strong tie to him, to enhance the bond between the two of you?"

"Yes, something like that."

"Well, 'something like that,' is what I'll explore then. As you know, I've got plenty of reading time where I 'live' now. What I'll do is, try to come up with a sort of 'moon-link.' Your mom's name means *born at the return of the moon,* and you're *her* daughter; also, you and Nashoba were *howling at the moon.* I'll look for a connection between all of that and attempt to concoct a spell. How does that sound?"

Erika grinned, practically giddy. "It sounds wonderful!"

"All right, I'll do it. I love you – see you soon, my cousin," said Emily, hugging Erika fiercely as she turned to go.

As she walked away, Erika heard Emily utter some form of chant, and as she did, disappeared from sight.

Chapter 16
Charissa

North Carolina, 1794 — The Mermaid nosed its way between other sailing ships to find a spot at the Port of Wilmington, along the Carolina coast. Under normal circumstances, arrivals from London would have gone to New York, but I'd brokered my way onto a ship transporting not only the likes of Quakers, German Lutherans, and Scottish-Irish Presbyterians, but it had also diverted to pick up a load of African slaves to take to the Americas. As such, it's port of call wound up being a good deal farther south than that of a routine passenger route. When you needed to leave home in a hurry and didn't have much money for fare, you had to take what you could get. I didn't want to go to my parents for help as this fiend I'd become.

The Mermaid had anchored, and I couldn't wait to get off this boat, having been surrounded by these religious sheep for what seemed like months at sea. Not that I wasn't familiar with lengthy sea travel by this point, but I'd mostly lost my taste for those of faith, considering what I'd been through – *and* what I'd turned into. *Why* I'd had to leave my homeland in the first place. But of course, that was all on me.

Speaking of 'taste,' sustenance had been tricky, considering my unique dietary needs now. I'd not wanted to embark upon another murder spree in the small world of an ocean ship, so I needed to get creative along the way. I'd mostly gone for 'little snacks' off of sleeping slaves when I was able. There were a couple of occasions where this didn't work out and they woke up while I was feeding. In those cases, I *did* end them, quietly mind you, then disposed of the body overboard in quick fashion before anyone was the wiser. Naturally, other slaves soon noticed their mates had turned up missing, but no slave traders were going to care – not until their numbers came up short upon debarking. And by then, I was long gone. However, if this 'new life' was going to work for me here in the new world, I was going to *have* to come up with better ways to manage myself besides more serial killing.

It was curious to note that, in those circumstances where the slave would wake up during my consumption, the moans emanating from him could well have been interpreted by others as the sounds of intercourse, considering I was female and on top of him. That got me thinking. Integrate my feeding somehow *as though it were* the sex act – as a decoy? *What am I thinking?* I thought as my mind did the progressive math. It appeared as if I was talking about prostituting myself! Considering my prudishness with regards to 'lovemaking' even *within* the context of a relationship, I could not see myself doing that at all.

Then again, before all of *this,* I wouldn't have dreamt of killing a bug – and look at me now. But no, even so, I felt like I was somehow on the right track with this; not a whore, dancer, or even an escort – but

something in between? But what would that be? I knew there had to be something, I just couldn't think of what it was. Well, later for that. I needed to look into transportation beyond here. I was not prepared to stay in this sea of Presbyterians, Lutherans and Quakers. I came for the so-called pursuit of 'life, liberty and the pursuit of happiness,' not more religious dogma. I'd had more than my fill.

My assimilation of information about this new territory I found myself in led me to the knowledge of an area called Tennessee, or Franklin as it was called in its rejected first bid for statehood. Initially a part of this *North Carolina*, it was further inland and more isolated, exactly what I was after. I set about looking for wagon transport to get there, which also proved to be a bit of an undertaking; but nothing compared to the seafaring journeys I'd already endured.

Besides what my food requirements were as this cannibal-vampire creature, I also found that I had a distinct aversion to the daylight. I'd break out, become weak, and feel as though I would wither away. A state I'd chosen to avoid as best I could. As such, *enclosed* travel to the likes of ships and carriages were definitely my preferred methods to journey. I found a coach route out of Wilmington within the week, which rounded its way northwest within 'treaty' lands to Knoxville. From there, it was covered wagon through Cherokee Indian territory until returning to the settlers' land in Nashville. After that, I'd decided to head towards what appeared to be the borderlands between another of the indigenous peoples, the Chickasaws, and those colonists' who would eventually oust them from their lands. Ahh, my native Europeans! Leaving their own oppression only to become the oppressors themselves. Not so unlike our Caribbean journey which

was likely the precursor to the removal of the cannibals. God, why couldn't I have been sent to visit *these* natives instead of those monsters?

Pondering this, I couldn't help suddenly feeling more drawn to the area than I was already. Perhaps I'd encounter a native culture who weren't beasts, and the circle of my life would loop back round toward some ironic redemption? Well, one could dream as the miles passed by – to Clarksville.

Chapter 17

Emily

Kate knocked hard upon the door leading down to Emily's basement 'living quarters,' announcing her descent into her 'liar.' An appropriate word considering that mother was now mostly aware of the 'crafting' her daughter had been up to.

"Em?" Kate called, going down.

"Right here, Mother," Emily answered, beckoning her. "I'm glad to see you. What brings you to the 'bad girl's den?"

"Well, darling, besides bringing lunch, *you do* – and what you've been up to, specifically. I believe I'm fairly certain that you've been coming and going of your own accord out of here – I've *sensed* you as you've passed to and fro, though no one else sees anything when you do. You've clearly learned a cloaking spell I'd say. Where did you go the other day?"

"Out to meet my cousin and Uncle Jed, Mom," she replied, making no attempt to hide a thing. "I've a direct connection to her now through her wolf – spirit animal. It's all very 'Indian,' dreamcatchers and such. The wolf wears one *as a collar* – and it's been the perfect talisman to re-open our dreaming to each other again."

"I see," answered Kate, understanding everything perfectly. "This *is not* the way I would have had you come into powers, given the choice."

"'Given the choice,' would have had me come into them at all, Mother?"

"Probably not. But things have happened as they have, and you've obviously found and been learning from the grimoires, correct?"

"Yes, Ma'am. I'm sorry, but when I was first punished down here years ago, I stumbled across them. I learned in short order that they were yours, and I honestly couldn't think of anything better to do while I was stuck here. Besides, it helped me get to better know you – the *you* you used to be."

"They weren't meant to be discovered," Kate said bluntly.

"Then you probably should've destroyed them, don't you think?" Emily questioned, taking a bite of food.

"I suppose so – " Kate trailed off.

"Well, they *weren't,* and, as you say, 'things have happened as they have,' so there's very little we can do to change any of that now."

"'Little,' darling – but not *nothing.* You *can* back off from your practices presently, inasmuch as you're going to be released soon. I've been working on him, and your father is soon to lift your punishment to this God forsaken hole."

"Really?" Emily said with interest. "That's wonderful. But – it doesn't mean I'm going to stop seeing Erika. She's coming to *me* now, not like before when I'd go search for *her.*"

"That's an improvement, but still very risky, daughter," Kate said, sighing.

"I *know,* Mother," Emily emphasized in reply, "but he's been doing this to me – to *us* – our whole lives, and I'm practically grown now. I just can't stay under his thumb anymore!

"You could pretend to in order to 'smooth' things – and keep *us* safe. Not to mention for Erika's and Jed's sakes as well."

"Always, Mother, of course. But I *can* stand up to him now, if it comes to that."

"Perhaps, Em. But he's still your father. You should respect that."

"So I keep hearing. Uncle Jed reminded me of this recently also. All right, I promise I will do my best."

"Your best *behavior* – *not* your best spells, yes?"

"Yes, Mom, I'll 'behave,'" Emily sighed in surrender.

Prior to Kate's dismissing herself and returning upstairs, their kitchen servant pulled away her listening ear from what she'd overheard below, scurrying away to report later to Robert what she'd just learned...

Chapter 18

Charissa

larksville – Now that I'd arrived at the place I presumed to do likewise as the immigrants; *settle* – I wasn't quite sure what to do with myself. Up until this moment, I'd been on mission to escape what had been wrought from my previous 'mission,' which was the result of the mission before that! It was all 'in the books' finally, and I found myself saying, 'what now'?

The earlier financial difficulties I'd encountered with respect to paying my travel fares and such were not nearly the problem they once were. It seemed as though there were upsides to this creature I'd become. Yes, daytime and the blood diet were cumbersome to say the least, but a particular ability to *influence* people – almost commanding anyone to do almost whatever I needed – seemed to be asserting itself with growing effectiveness. I'd noticed it more frequently since arriving to this country. I'd inquire as to a route, mode of travel, or a destination, and the travel broker would dismiss any notion on my part of being short of fare. They would say, 'don't worry, we'll work it out upon arrival;' then say 'on the house' when we got there. I thought it was dumb luck at first, but once a regular pattern began to emerge, it appeared there was definitely something to it.

I'd decided to put it to the test to see if it was real or not. During layovers in a given town, I'd order a meal I didn't really need, or inquire as to lodging. In all cases, I was waved along when payment exchange would normally have been expected. I started paying heed to my tone and word usage. I began to see that the more I *'told'* over *'asked,'* the more efficiently this control I had seemed to work. I wished I'd realized it sooner, actually. Had I known what I could do with it, the feeding practices on-ship that had encountered hiccups might've gone much smoother. I could have *willed* my victims to be docile while partaking of them, thus avoiding those unsavory results of 'a snack gone wrong.' Alas, life, even 'un-life' is ever a learning curve.

This new-found skill proved to be a boon. It allowed me, almost immediately, to procure employ at the local tavern and lodge in the midst of town. I'd managed both income and a roof in one fell swoop. The compromise, however, was that I was reduced to being that of a 'saloon girl,' pushing drinks and entertaining men. I'd surely 'found something to do with myself,' though certainly not at all what I had in mind. But, since I was still in the midst of figuring out this new life, I was mostly content to make do. In many cases, *more* was expected of me than just serving them drinks and being flirtatious. Not really a problem though, inasmuch as I could take them to my room, have them *believe* they'd had their way with me, and get a little meal out of it in the process.

Still, all things in moderation was my motto. If I acquiesced to being too much their 'regular,' that would establish a reputation I didn't

want. If I made too many meals out of patrons, word would easily get around that customers often came away with bites from the 'lady Charissa.' It was from this dilemma it occurred that a 'broader menu' than only human should be made.

So, around dusk one day when I didn't have a night's shift ahead of me, I gazed out across the wilderness beyond the borders of town. I mused that 'the lady Charissa' might do well to become 'Charissa the huntress' – seeking out wild game for sustenance. It certainly wasn't that I hadn't been such previously anyway, with the bishops. As I proceeded to stroll into the forestland ahead, I thought I'd observed the lithe figure of a girl making its way back to the outermost house of town. I watched her curiously, not entirely sure why – I was simply intrigued. I quickly noticed also, that an animal had followed her in trail. When she reached a certain threshold towards the house, the creature turned-tail and went back from whence it had come. As she approached the home and the animal continued its retreat the opposite direction, I advanced. I reached the place where they had separated and stood there for a moment.

Now, I am by no means an expert, but the experience that led me to this wretched existence was initiated by a shaman practicing a filthy, dark magic. And while I stood in this spot, I felt as though I sensed something similar afoot. Magic – but it didn't feel as though it were cut out of the same cloth from which I was made. It felt, I don't know, earthen, spiritual – pure. It was 'good' somehow. Suddenly, I wanted to follow one of them, one direction or the other. Since I was originally heading towards the forest and possible prey, I chose to follow what I now surmised to be a wolf. How ironic, a vampire tracking a lycan.

It had gotten a good lead on me by the time I'd finished feeling the magic aura of where they'd parted, so I picked up my pace. Soon, I'd found myself amazed at my own speed in closing the gap. It appeared I'd discovered yet another extraordinary prowess of this thing I'd become. Now, curious upon curious, the wolf in the distance seemed to have returned to yet *another* girl. Were I 'normal,' I would not have been able to distinguish in the fading light any details of the female the beast had gone to, but *I could* clearly see she was of the native descent. So, I was into the Indians' land now, but that was neither here nor there. I wasn't sure what to make of all of this. A wolf escorting *one* girl back home, then returning to another who was probably its master, judging by the way they moved on together. Were the girls connected through the wolf? By magic? Or both? It appeared that they may well have come from meeting one another – that is, if any my intuitions were right.

I wasn't going to find out anything more about these three tonight, but I decided then and there that they would become my new distraction to my absurd life back in town. In the meantime, I had originally come out here this night perhaps to hunt – and it was time to get to it. The woods were invigorating – it reminded me of the first time I'd become aware of my heightened senses of sight, smell and hearing back in the Caribbean. Aside from my ocean travels, I hadn't been out in nature like this since the island, and I was relishing it.

In short order, I'd targeted a deer, taken it, and made it a meal. Not bad for a first outing, and not horrible to the palette, but certainly not as good as human. Speaking of which, I encountered yet *one* more person as I made my way back to Clarksville. I don't know how much

time had elapsed between seeing the girls, following the wolf, and procuring my deer, but it didn't seem like very long to me. As such, when I saw *the man,* it struck me that he could well have appeared in the *wake* of the girls. I don't know why I felt this, but in the rather short span of time in between all their appearances, I couldn't imagine him being out here and *not* somehow connected to them.

What had gotten into me? Had the London inspectors of my crimes rubbed off on me? Taken me to the place of all manner of deductions? *Gracious, I must finally be cracking,* I thought. Regardless, I determined I was absolutely going to stay on 'this case.' Perhaps it would actually *help* keep my sanity. And just maybe – lead me to others – like myself.

Chapter 19
Em – Erika

Robert had at last granted Emily's release from his punishment of forcing her to live in the basement for a month. Their relationship was now worn and strained due to the experience. Neither interacted with each other in anywhere near the same manner they used to. For Robert's part, he no longer monitored her with the iron fist he had previously. Instead, he utilized the spotty information his slave-woman, Clare, had gathered and reported to him. Her vantage-point in eavesdropping had not been the best, and had really only gotten that Emily and the Indian cousin would seek to rendezvous at random, unknown times.

To that, Robert had taken to trying to track Emily's movements outside the house. No easy task as Em continued to utilize her cloaking spells to mask when she left the premises. It would be a good while before he would meet with much progress to his efforts. But, unbeknownst to any of them in their comings and goings, they were *all* now being observed – by *another.*

This other would also tend to mirror Robert's odds at success as *her* times to survey were limited to the evening. It wasn't that Emily and Erika never came together later in the day; after all, it had been then when *her* awareness of them all had first come. But most often they met during the day, not an ideal time for their new pursuer. This *one* did, however, have a singular advantage over Robert as *she* could see through Emily's spell cloaks, whereas he could not. Thus it went for Robert and their shadowed, secret stalker – quite the game of hit and miss, cat and mouse.

. . . .

Emily and Erika engaged in a number of things when they came together. They talked greatly, catching up on all of their lives they'd missed growing up. They spoke also of the magics Em was learning and Erika's tribal culture – and where the two intersected. Without having to push for it, they discovered an almost natural relationship between the two practices, and sought to integrate them when and where they could. This was mostly towards the ultimate goal of bonding Erika and Nashoba to a greater depth than they already were – and the girls *were* close – close to enacting a spell.

The other thing they liked to do was hunt together. Emily's earlier vision when she'd first shared connection to Nashoba and the dream collar had become a reality. The bow and the rifle had come together. And *this* – would be their Achilles heel. Generally, once the girls had made their rendezvous on any given day, Emily would drop her cloak, in order for Erika to see her. They'd be far enough from the Clarksville area that they weren't worried about getting caught. All logical, *except* for Em's ignorance to the fact her father *was* trying to track them, spy on them, and see what they were up to.

Now, though Robert was at a distinct disadvantage in this, it was from their hunting that he would get a leg up. Any time, for example, when Emily had vanished and Robert had stalked out to look for her, it would be from *her **shot*** fired that he'd finally gain an edge. The first time, naturally, had been a fluke. He could not have known from whom it came – it could've been anyone. But, when subsequent shots followed, he was able to move closer to the direction of the sound. When he'd gotten near enough and found it to be her, he used the same tactic from then on in his surveillance of the girls.

Why had he gone from *dictator* over his daughter, laying down the law and simply meting out punishments when it was broken – to *this*? Because the former wasn't working any longer, and it had broken them. She was nearly grown now, and would to continue to resist him. There was something different about her now, something more confident and brazen. The only way to break this down, he thought, would be to get to its core, the dammed half-breed cousin. This would take a patience he was not used to having, but have it he would, for the 'greater good.'

• • • •

At last the day came when Emily felt ready – for the bonding spell of her cousin to her wolf. Together, Em and Erika had studied dutifully from the sides of both magic and the tradition of the Chickasaw in an effort to achieve a specific and personal invocation. All was ready; the three of them were gathered together, and the full moon had begun to rise in the dusk of the day's end. Also, they'd chosen the month of Erika's birth as this was what made her spirit animal the wolf. They'd

come to a familiar spot, one that had become theirs over time.

It was the same area Robert was tracking towards this night as well, as he no longer required a gunshot to lead him to where they were. He'd come to know their patterns and places, and had logged them in his mind. He'd been a little late getting underway, having dozed off a spell after supper, then realized Emily had gone – again. He'd told Kate he'd had a few duties to attend to in the supply shed – slipping out to anywhere but.

. . . .

Emily had drawn a circle in the ground to depict the moon, seating Erika and Nashoba in its center. A second dreamcatcher collar had also been crafted, more of a necklace really, for Erika to wear for the rite as well. Cousin and wolf synced with their respective talismans, the girls hummed a Chickasaw tribal chant, followed by Emily's pronouncement of the spell itself.

"Born at the return of the moon," she began, "and weaned by spirit of the wolf, may this *beskwa* be taken into the cycle of Luna – to the heart of her Choctaw. May his instincts be hers, and hers, his. Bring the scent and the way of the hunt into them both, as *one* – for ever and always. As moon circles earth, may their rings ever revolve, round and round – and round again."

For its final completion, the spell required a certain element of – *blood* – as a 'bonding agent.' In a fashion akin to any playful roughhousing between human and pet, Erika began vigorously roughing Nashoba's fur at the crick of his neck. Deliberately, she got a free hand near his jawline as she did. Moving her face in close to his, she gingerly blew

into his snout. Dogs, by nature not caring much for this, gave a light bite into her closely-lingering hand. Nashoba drew back, lapping the blood drops he'd drawn onto his pallet, and briefly swallowed. He then came back to the bitten hand, licking it clean, honoring his alpha. And so, it was done.

Hidden, Robert had seen it all.

Further behind him – Charissa had too.

Chapter 20

Charissa

I had been absolutely, one hundred percent right. They *were* magic – both of them! The Indian girl trying to apply her culture's spiritual beliefs into a deeper bond with her animal. The American girl clearly dedicated to learning this craft of hers, helping the *skwa* make that happen. And then – there was that man. He gave *me,* of all people, chills. The way he followed them. Watched them. I had been correct on that account too – he *was* connected to them. It didn't take being Sherlock Holmes to deduce he was probably the white girl's father. Of course, *I* was watching all of them – nothing suspicious to my own character there! No, of course not.

I'd not been able to scout about to look in on them nearly as much as I would have liked. Many nights, when I wasn't stuck with a shift at the tavern, I would try to get out and find them; but no surprise, I'd find nothing. However magic they might be, they were still young, human girls who wouldn't be out wandering the woods at night. Except for this night. The one they'd chosen to attempt a spell by the bright moonlight. The night I'd been blessed with the pure, dumb luck of finding them again. Though I don't say this often anymore, Thank God I saw what I did this evening. The touching, intriguing moment of the spell-cast aside, the important thing to have glimpsed was *him* spying on them. There was *nothing* good going to come from that man having observed it. I knew it in my soul – or whatever piece of one I still had.

I had this feeling he was, somehow, a danger to them. Yes, he *was* visibly father to one of them, so that *shouldn't* be. Still, I couldn't shake it. Now I felt like I had to make an even stronger effort to look out for them. The question was, how? How was I ever going to reach them when they were mostly together during the day? Perhaps the little witch could cast some kind of 'daylight' spell for me – but I'd *have to find* her again for that! In retrospect, I probably should have introduced myself the first time I saw her. I'm sure that would have gone famously; a strange woman as disturbing than the 'father-stalker' – and far more dark and deadly.

Who was I fooling? These girls didn't need me; they would probably get along just fine among themselves. The Indian had the wolf, the white girl, her magic – *and* an intrinsic bond betweenst them all. More than formidable enough for the petty man. I could not have been more wrong.

. . . .

Chapter 21

Erika

Days had passed since the spell-binding Emily had cast for Erika and Nashoba. It remained a tad early to tell how well it had worked, but Erika was seeing clear enough signs to satisfy her. She was experiencing a heightened sense of awareness into Nashoba's thoughts and instincts. She understood to a much greater degree the communication in the howls, whines, growls or barks coming from him. And she felt that he too, could better grasp the human words, tones and inflections of her respective language.

When together in the woods for a hunt, they worked in unison as a team better than ever before. They had become their own small pack unto themselves. On such a day, they rendezvoused with Emily once more, the completion of their 'pack' grouping. Erika shared their progress with her, and Em was ecstatic. Not only insofar as to their improvement with one another, but also to her own confidence as far as how well she was advancing in her practice of her art. They left each other that day on a high note, both immensely satisfied and feeling blessed for their coming together after all the years apart.

. . . .

Erika and Nashoba were on their way back from their time with Emily – when they both sensed, together, that they were being followed. Her first thought, naturally, was that her cousin had forgotten something and doubled back. "Em?" she called out.

"Close," came a voice – similar after a fashion, but lower in register, male, older. Robert.

"Show yourself!" cried Erika, while Nashoba growled. Quickly turning to him, she shushed the wolf, gesturing for him to circle around to remain hidden – and poised. He did so as Robert emerged from a stand of trees, arms apart as though to say, 'no threat.'

"I am your *cousin's* father," he said, accenting distaste in the word 'cousin.'

"I know who you are," Erika replied with equal disdain. "Why do you follow me – alone – apart from your daughter? If you've found me, you've had ample opportunity to come to us *both* together, yet you seek me out by myself. Why?"

"Because I wish to talk with you – alone."

"I asked you *why!*" she snapped.

"Because I need to stress to *you* that I do not care for your influence upon Emily. I have seen what you both have been up to with your strange Indian practices in the night. I am here to tell you to stop."

"What?" said Erika in utter disbelief of the man's blatant ignorance and blindness.

"You heard me fine, squaw. I don't believe I stuttered. Emily has been spiraling towards these strange behaviors for as long as she's been making efforts to see you – and that has been for, God, years I now realize. She's duped me for longer than I care to admit, and

despite my punishments to put a stop to it, she *still* makes her way out here to be with you. I've left alone my turncoat brother to you and yours – and now you must do the same. Leave Emily alone!"

Erika could not believe her ears. He was literally blaming *everything* about his daughter he could no longer control – *on her!* Especially, it seemed, the witchcraft; which Em had learned entirely apart from her, all on her own. Now, this too, was 'Erika's fault.' Convenient, because she was a different race, a different belief system than his own. What to do? If she stood up for herself, revealing what Em was becoming in the process, she'd be selling her cousin completely down the river. If she said nothing, she'd be helping add ever more seeds to the man's blindness and bigotry.

Finally, she said, "I believe you need to look more inwardly than from without for your answer, sir. Emily would be pushing apart from you regardless of my presence or beliefs."

"What is that supposed to mean?" barked Robert, unable to see the forest from the trees.

"I am saying that *I* am not the cause of Emily's behaviors that you no longer understand – *you are!*"

"How dare you, child!" he scolded. "It is not I, but the Lord God himself who commands that peoples keep to themselves and not intersperse amongst one another! *This* is why I'll not brook my brother's matrimony with your mother, nor *you* with my daughter! I can be no clearer – *do not* come to her again!" he shouted with hand raised and finger pointed in her face.

And that was all it took.

Nashoba burst from his cover, lunging towards Robert unexpectedly.

Bowling the man over, the wolf's forward momentum shot him past Robert for a brief moment's span. As Nashoba turned about to re-engage, Robert scrambled for his pistol. As he prepared to fire, Erika, in defense to her loyal friend, moved in between them – taking the shot meant for the wolf. It hit her squarely in the chest, directly to her heart. She dropped immediately, grasping for Nashoba. He wanted to keep after the man, tear him limb from limb, but the bond to his alpha so much more enhanced as it now was, overrode the killer instinct.

Robert was in shock, his mind a blur, his bumbling hand dropping the gun. As adamant as he'd been to his goal in shutting down Emily's relations to the Indian mutt, *this* result had never been on the table whatsoever. Nashoba continued to growl at him menacingly, but remained at his master's wounded side. He dared not approach the beast, no telling what the wolf would do to him at the slightest move. Not seeing any other options open to him considering the circumstances, he backed away, retrieved the gun, returned to his feet and went his way – basically leaving the girl behind, for dead.

She *wasn't* yet – but was fading fast. "Nash, my brother, my spirit," Erika said brokenly, "come close." She pinched her hand into the fur of his neck, holding tight. "I am you – you are me. I put all of myself into *you* now. Once I *am,* take me to Em in the dreaming place. But we must not show her – *this.* At least, not how it has come about. She and her father will *never* recover if she knows. Ease my family's pain to my departure – but find a way to let them know – I'm *in* you."

With that, her grip upon him loosened, her hand dropped, and her body – stopped. Stopped breathing, blood flowing, eyes seeing – motor functioning. With mortal host no longer viable, her *spirit* – went to –

animal.

Nashoba howled loudly both in pain – and in victory. For it *was* one, of sorts. The wolf had become complete with his human – she was *fully* integrated into him now – and this was good. Yet, at the same time, lay before them, her lifeless body, and that was – not. Nashoba whirled to return to the village of the Chickasaws.

. . . .

Somberly, Nashoba doubled back to this 'place of passing,' having come back from the village in order to bring Jed to recover Erika. Jed fell to his knees in grief next to her body, not believing what he was seeing. "Oh my darling," he cried in pain, "no, oh *no!* How has this happened?" he bewailed, beginning to notice that it looked like she'd been shot.

Almost immediately, Nashoba nudged Jed's elbow with his snout, then offered a paw upon his wrist. If he didn't know better, Jed could've sworn that it felt like the touch of his daughter's hand. The wolf caught his gaze and nodded as though answering 'yes.' Jed blinked in dismay, not daring to believe what he perceived *could* be happening. Nashoba then reached to put his other paw to Jed's opposite arm, thereby pulling himself into Jed, as if to 'hug' him. And there, with their heads moving forward together to touch, Jed *knew* and felt that Erika was indeed – still here.

. . . .

Chapter 22

Charissa

Something was different that evening as I'd begun the night's shift at the tavern. I'd felt a kind of disturbance to my normal sleep pattern through the course of the day, before work. I'd awoken here and there to dream splinters of a wolf leaping from the woods, a shot fired, and someone falling – dead. This was interspersed with my more routine imagery of cardinals and bishops lying drained and dead, James with his throat ripped open, and Andrea biting her way through 'un-life' just as I did. All together, I assumed that my life from before and my life now were simply coalescing in nightmarish unison, giving me my just desserts for all that I'd done to earn their torments.

However, as I entered the establishment and prepared myself for my duties, I observed the presence of one who *never* frequented here whatsoever. But there *he* was at the bar, getting fully inebriated. The man in the woods. The father of the young witch. Upon my identification of him, something snapped in my mind, bringing into focus from whose gun the shot had been fired in my dream. *His.*

As the night wore on, he remained. As I served patrons and flirted, I kept open a keen ear to his meandering conversation with the barkeep. He was clearly beside himself about something, and the longer he blithered on, the more certain I was becoming as to what it was. He'd done *something* – bad. Akin to the likes of things I'd done, I sensed somehow. After a bit came the clincher. At the point when his drunkenness had reached its pinnacle, I overheard him bemoan, "I shouldn't have left her! But, the wolf – "

And with that said, all the puzzle pieces from my dreams fit together. It was towards *him* the wolf had lunged. Not a random wolf, but the one *belonging to* the girls. The shot fired was to fell *it*. But the one who *was* felled dead was, dear Father in Heaven – the Indian girl! The *wolf's* girl. I staggered, as though intoxicated myself, in realization. I nearly dropped my serving tray with a fresh load of drinks when it hit me. Now I, like he, was beside myself. My mishap had not gone unnoticed, neither by a good portion of the customers, nor by him.

"Are you all right, miss?" he slurred to my direction.

"I'll be fine," I answered, needing a moment. Placing the platter to the side, I returned gaze to his and the barkeep's direction, and asked, "May I be excused a minute, please?" Having said it in a manner more statement than question, no one took issue as I'd asserted *my will*. I stepped to the back in attempt to try and process all that I'd just surmised.

The sheer magnitude of the moment struck me like a ton of bricks. If any or all of this were true, I'd surely let those girls down. I'd convinced myself that these lasses didn't need any aid from some foreign murderess-creature such as myself. But, if these things indeed *had* occurred, then I'd absolutely shirked a duty placed upon me – by having been privy to the unfolding events I'd observed in watching them. Some deed on my part that could've been my act of redemption might've been at hand, and instead I'd shied away for fear of the daylight.

Yet, despite the fact this was a clear case of 'too little, too late,' a secondary opportunity might well be presenting itself. One that I *had* to be willing to take this time. So, having regained my composure, I returned to the front. I made quick work of seeing to delivery of the drinks I'd left at my station, apologizing to everyone for my momentary lapse. In typical fashion, my charm deferred any lingering impatience by the patrons for their late drinks.

Now I turned attention again to my 'person of interest.' Sidling up to the bar next to him, I returned his courtesy from before and asked, "What of you, sir? Are *you* all right? Are you fine to make it back home? As I've not seen you here before, I wonder if you've not overextended yourself?"

The barkeep looked at me cross as if I should keep my nose out of it and let him keep slinging drinks. I glared back, ending any point of contention between us. God, this ability was grand!

"I confess that I normally do not drink like this," he said after a pause, letting loose a whiskey-laddened burp. "I've had something of a bad day, and couldn't return home and put on 'a normal face' for everyone – not without a distraction first. So, I came here – to commiserate."

"And drink beyond your limits, perhaps?" I offered.

To this, he first lightly chuckled – then bellowed out with laughter. Despite being off-put by his stalking the girls *and* what I now suspected he'd done, I had to admit, I didn't mind his *drunken* self! I found myself laughing along with him. And this was a good step towards making him comfortable with me.

Because next, I took it a step further, earning yet another burning glare from the barback.

"Yeeesss," I giggled with him, "one *must* know their limits. As you've exceeded yours, good sir, allow me to help you on home." To which he first waved his hand as though unnecessary. But, in a stumbled attempt to rise from his stool, he again chuckled – and gave in to my offer.

"*Charissa* – " uttered the bartender in a clearly objective tone, looking to put a stop to me leaving with him.

"You'll be fine," I said, looking at him squarely, compelling him to that fact. "You'll handle the place perfectly while I'm gone. I shan't be long." I had no idea *how long* I was going to be, and I didn't care. My goal here was to get whatever else I could out of him – and to, hopefully, have a long overdue face-to-face – with his daughter, the little witch.

I didn't get much out of him on the way home. He may have been drunk out of his mind, but he was surely smart enough, even in this state, not to give anything *truly* incriminating away. He didn't in the pub, nor did he now. It didn't matter. I'd heard all I'd needed to regardless. Besides, he was mostly just a segue to get me in front of the girl anyway.

• • • •

Chapter 23
Emily

Soon, at the Laydons' homestead, came a long overdue knock upon the door. It was late, around nine o'clock, but it didn't take long for Kate to come and answer. She'd been worriedly waiting up, wondering where Robert could be. She was shocked, not only to see her husband grossly inebriated, but also to the unexpected presence of a strange woman accompanying him home.

"What's happened to him?" exclaimed Kate, receiving Robert into her arms as Charissa handed him off. "And *who* ever might you be, young miss?"

"Please pardon me, ma'am," Charissa began in very proper English dialect, setting Kate immediately more at ease. "My name is Charissa Westcott, and I am of employ at the tavern in town. I assure you, your husband is the farthest thing from a regular in our establishment. As I have never seen him before tonight, I deemed he might do well with some aid home, considering his present condition."

"Thank you, Miss Westcott, you are – very thoughtful," Kate said with pause, still somewhat reeling from this most unusual situation. That is to say, unusual *for them*. As Kate pulled Robert further inside, Emily suddenly appeared there by her side, edging her way into their midst. Though surprised that she was up, Kate took advantage of her presence, asking if she could please stay with lady while she put Robert to bed.

"Of course, Mother," answered Emily, while looking Charissa over with scrutinous interest. "I was restless tonight," she explained, "and overheard the noise at the door."

"Thank you, dear," Kate called back satisfied, receding towards the bedrooms with Robert.

"So – " began Emily, now fully focused upon the stranger in their doorway, "I heard you say that you brought Father home from the tavern – and you work there?"

"That is correct, lass," Charissa replied, "my apologies for the disturbance; I simply felt he would do well to have some help getting home." She paused with breath before segueing into what she would say next.

"You say you've been restless this night, miss? Ironically, I found myself much the same way before work, while *I* tried also to slumber. Given the similarity, may I ask what troubled *you?*"

"First of all," she began, "My name is Emily, and I heard you tell Mom that you're Charissa. Hello. Secondly, I've been restless over my cousin, who I saw earlier today. But tonight, since then, I've been feeling unusually worried about her – and I'm concerned as to why."

"*Your cousin,* you say?" Charissa returned, surprised to hear of the *familial* connection between the two. "Forgive me for asking, Emily, but is your cousin an Indian girl?"

"She *is* – how – *why* would you ask, Charissa? What could you possibly know of that?"

Charissa knew her next words were pivotal and she would need to choose them carefully and precisely. "Because, dear girl, tonight is *not* the first time I've been aware of your father – nor of you *or* your cousin."

She was about to elaborate, but Emily cut her to the quick, asking, "What exactly are you saying, 'dear lady'?"

"I am *saying* that I have observed you from a distance previously – and I am aware of your magic – for I myself am cursed – with a *dark* magic. I *will not* get into that as that is my burden, not yours. But, I need you to know that my concern *is* for you and your cousin. I've seen you both, *and* your wolf too. I can only hope you might believe me."

At that point, most sane persons might well have slammed the door in Charissa's face, but instead, Emily seized the woman's hand – and squeezed. Hard. Closing her eyes, utilizing all she'd learned of magic's ways up till now, she felt for Charissa's sincerity – as well as this 'dark magic' she spoke of. Sensing it immediately, Em quickly released her hand, but out of courtesy, only withdrew slowly.

"Well?" Charissa asked, her breath catching, fearful of what Emily may have gleaned.

"Well – I feel your darkness plainly," Em shivered, "and I agree, it's best kept to yourself. But, you do not lie when you say you're concerned for me – and mine. Tell me, how do you come to know of us? Are you some kind of spy?"

Charissa couldn't help but laugh for a second – a 'spy.' "No, my dear, not that. Though I suppose with the way I have come to seek, and look out *for* you, it certainly does amount to that. The simple truth is, one

day before taking a stroll into the woods, I saw you from a distance. I saw the wolf follow you part way home, then turn about and go back – to *her.* I walked to the spot where you'd separated and sensed the magic residue left behind in your wake; just as you've now sensed the dark magic within me. I assure you, I am not such as yourself, I am the *result* of a shaman's filthy magic cast *upon* me. It has banished me to be a creature of *only* the night; thus I've not been able to check on you both during the course of the days. And throughout *this* day, I've been troubled by something I've felt is very wrong – with respect to your Indian."

"'Wrong – as though," Emily choked knowingly, "she may have – left us?"

Charissa felt urged to reach back and hold Emily's hand again as she responded, "Yes – *you've* felt this too then."

This had been a huge risk in coming here at all, Charissa thought, let alone this level of honesty. At this juncture, she felt it would be pushing her luck completely to share her near-certainty of the father's involvement to it, so she chose to say nothing more. At least for now.

Emily took advantage of Charissa's musing pause and said, "I'm going out there early on the morrow then – to the Chickasaw lands. Before anyone here is awake to stop me. I must go see what's happened. I have to know. I know I just met you, but clearly, you've connected to us in some strange way. I would ask you to come along, but you've said you cannot go in the daylight, so I won't. I hope it is not too forward to say, but I wish that you *could* go with."

"I wish I could too," Charissa said, realizing they were still holding hands.

Emily was also cognizant of this as she offered, again squeezing Charissa's hand, "As it seems you are open to dreams, I will try to 'send' one to you – to tell you of what I learn. And, if you like, a call to return to me betweenst there and here – *in the night.*"

Charissa smiled to this, taking her other hand out to cusp Emily's hand in both of her's. She'd been right – she *had* met someone like herself. Far more innocent than she, but a sort-of kindred nonetheless.

It was then Kate had at last returned, in the midst of what looked like their parting to her. "I apologize for taking so long, ladies," she began. "Thank you Em, for entertaining our guest. Charissa, thank you so much for bringing Robert home. I don't know how he would have fared alone."

"You are more than welcome," replied Charissa. "We *do* have to look out for the patrons after all. Besides, your daughter is a dear. I hope we cross paths again," she said in conclusion, glancing at Kate, but looking squarely at Emily, as if in response to what Em proposed before Kate's return.

Yes, dream to me, thought Charissa.

Emily nodded affirmatively.

Chapter 24

Erika

It had been a mournful night in the village of the Chickasaw across the forestlands from Clarksville. The tribe had lost one of their own and were overcome with grief. At least one member of the community was not convinced, however, that she was indeed 'lost.' It was Jed, and with the dawn, he rose in that fact, to the hope of a new day. This hope greeted him almost immediately upon his emergence from slumber. Nashoba. Or, *Nasherka,* as he was beginning to think of the wolf now.

Before he'd returned with Erika's body yesterday, he'd cleaned it up for presentation as best he could; wiped away the blood, cleaned the gunshot wound. He'd removed the bullet to examine, having found it to be the kind and caliber he knew Robert to use in his guns. That alone meant nothing; many shooters used the same. Still, it certainly didn't dismiss his brother from suspicion either. Many settlers felt similar to Robert towards Indians; it could've been anyone. Yet, Robert's was the prejudice he knew *best* – and it was personal, specific to him and his. There was no getting around it – Robert *was,* above all others, at the top of the list. This was not over. But, later for that. Now was the time to let go; and explore a chance of something else – something hopefully not, so *final.*

Jed had not yet shared with Tanyee his intuition that their daughter might actually still exist *within* her animal. He felt a little time was needed to process first one thing, *then* another. And that time, as she came to him this morn, was now. He reached out his hand to take hers as she sat down next to him. He clasped it lovingly and kissed it before guiding it downward to pet Nashoba sitting beneath them. It was as natural as could be, and she took to caressing his fur unconsciously, completely on reflex.

"Close your eyes, my love," Jed whispered softly. "Keep petting Nash – and think of Erika," was all he said, or would say for the next few moments.

Tanyee thought it both odd and perhaps a tad cruel for Jed to *prompt* her to the rawness of her daughter's passing only a day removed. But she did as he asked anyway, just quietly petting their wolf – and thinking of the daughter she'd been blessed beyond measure to have. Minutes passed, followed by a sudden bolt of awareness of where Jed had been guiding her to. Tanyee flashed open her eyes, exclaiming, "Chepota!" She wheeled around from where she'd been seated over Nashoba, dropping to the ground in front of him. She looked at him dead on, grabbing his neck by the fur and roughing it in ecstasy. 'Nasherka's' snout protruded forward as the wolf began licking her face like there was no tomorrow.

"You *knew* of this?" she queried, looking to Jed. "And said nothing until now?"

"I strongly suspected. I felt as though bringing her back having

passed on was enough for one day. I wanted for that settle in first – then this."

"Please," she returned, "next time, tell me, right away. This would've helped."

Embracing her, he said, "I'm sorry, forgive me."

Having pulled away from Tanyee in that moment, the wolf bolted upright, as if in alert – to something else. He sniffed the air about him, yipped, and proceeded to run off into the woods. Surprised, the couple broke apart, wondering what it was all about.

"Let us go follow," Tanyee suggested. "That's our girl in him now too. And there's only one thing I can think of that takes them *both* into the forest like that."

Jed nodded in agreement, speaking in unison with his wife, *"Emily."*

· · · ·

Exactly as they'd surmised, Jed and Tanyee found Nashoba with Emily when they'd finally caught up to him, a short while later.

"Em!" Jed shouted to her as they approached. He'd expected her to come running to him upon calling out to her – but she didn't.

Despite Nashoba's prompts to her to do so, she remained crouched upon the ground, too engrained unto the details in the earth she seemed to be surveying. She was picking at a darkened, apparently stained area of the dirt. "Hello, uncle," she said, looking up at him, but staying stooped down. *"This* is where she was felled, yes? I see it, I feel it. Stronger even, than when it all came to me in dreams last night. I felt it as early as then that she'd gone into Nashoba here," she said, petting him next to her. "And as much as she's tried to mask it from me, I

sense my father was involved – just as I suspect *you* do also."

Jed was taken aback. He'd expected she might be an emotional muddle this early into the tragedy, but clearly not so. She was all business, cutting to the quick even, towards his own suspicions of his brother.

"Robert?" Tanyee queried in shock, looking to Jed in expectation of an answer.

"We do not *know* this, my love," his only offering for the moment. "But, it *is* within the realm of possibility."

"Probability," Emily corrected. "And *we* are not the only ones who think so. I made a friend last night who I sense may suspect him also, though she did not allude to it verbally. A barmaid who brought father home drunk from the tavern. Though she was courteous enough to bring him back, I've come to know that her goal was to meet *me* – more than her initial guise of 'looking out for him.' She's English, and is strangely cursed by a magic that limits her existence to the night. I don't understand it, but it *is,* somehow, the way she's been drawn to me – to *us;* Erika and Nashoba too, who are now one and the same. She's observed us all, before *this* happened; even Father's spying upon us. If not for being 'a *dark* angel,' one only able to be about at night, she'd have been our '*guardian* angel,' and would've intervened to *stop* Father – in the day, when it happened – if she could've."

"You sound as if you've put a lot of faith in someone you've only just met, Em," offered Jed. "How can you be so sure of someone who's come from out of nowhere?"

"I cannot be, of course," she came back, "but I tested her by the magic I've learned. I held her hand and looked inside – she *is* as sincere

to me as she claims – *and* as dark as she admits. She is troubled by a ghastly past, wishing only to connect with souls akin to herself – and do better."

"A soul such as *you,*" offered Tanyee. "But what of *your* father, whom you all so clearly suspect hurt my daughter in this way? When – and *what* do you plan to do about him?"

"I'll be going to confront my brother straightaway, Tanyee," Jed began, "I will – "

"No, Uncle, please," Emily begged, rising from the ground. "You're needed here with your family and your tribe. *You* and *I* – have things to attend to with respect to resurrecting Erika – fully. And I believe I know how. Besides, we now have *Charissa,* my new friend, who is perfectly positioned to exact justice upon my father, if necessary, back in Clarksville.

"You make it sound as though she were a demon you'd call upon to exact vengeance upon an enemy, Em," said Jed. "I thought you'd said she was your friend."

"She is, or at least, *will be.* All I know is, based on what I'd seen within her, she is more than able *and willing,* to make right, wrongs. I sensed too, that she's taken things to the extreme before, but wishes to get past being like that. And this is good. However, her clear mistrust of Father, combined with a kinship to me, makes her entirely balanced to do this, whatever, *this* may prove to be."

Jed and Tanyee sighed together to Em's assertions, their uneasiness being crystal clear.

"Please, you two, trust me. I know how doubtful it all seems, and *I* sound cold and calculating; but I simply trust this woman – and I've

grown confident in *my* abilities. She can do this – and so can I. You can meet her if you like. I intend to invite her out this way in the night before long, so that I may speak with her again – let her know what's become of Erika too. Besides me, she's come to care for her as well."

Apprehension remained in their faces, but Tanyee and Jed at last nodded a strained acknowledgement to the pronouncements of his eccentric-sounding niece.

Chapter 25
Charissa

I had returned to my work that night, after getting Emily's father safely back home. There were still customers enough to be dealt with, and luckily, at *least* a couple who were looking to 'get lucky' later. I was thankful to this as I'd worked up quite an appetite and was getting famished. Wrapping up at the pub after a couple hours more, I'd selected a gent to take back to my room with me, compelling him that I'd made him 'a happy man.' But instead, it was *I* who'd actually been satisfied – with a decent meal. After sending him out on his way about a half an hour later, I relaxed, pondering my newfound association with the young witch.

I wished it had been under better circumstances; that we'd not, presumably, lost the cousin; that her father hadn't gone down the same deadly road I've paved previously – in blood. But, presumably, he *had*. I truly hoped Emily would find better news when she traveled by early light to the Chickasaws. I would have loved more than anything to go with her, gone together *in the night;* but not knowing how I'd be received by the Indians *or* where I'd find sanctuary for the daytime, I just couldn't risk it. As it stood, perhaps I could help towards her ends *here,* around her family as some kind of liaison, so to speak, while she was away.

As dawn came and I prepared to hibernate, I was anxious. I found myself doing something I hadn't in quite some time. *I prayed* – that Emily would find some positive news out there, and that she'd be successful in 'dream-calling' to me. Show me something – *anything* that would keep me in the know. It wasn't easy to quiet myself down to rest, but at least I'd gotten full earlier, and that helped. I probably should have helped *that* man home too. Well, c'est la vie.

As dreams go, at least mine anyway, they tended to be disjointed, splintered, and these days, violent. So, when Emily's 'dream-channeling' reached me, the difference was stark. The first things that came to me were clear and concise images of the Indian girl and her wolf. The imagery was coalesced, intertwined to one another, and it was plain that they'd somehow – merged. I knew immediately that her spirit was now *in* the wolf. She *had* passed, yes; yet she lived on *within* the animal! I felt better, comforted. More than I could say for anyone I had killed – except of course, for Andrea.

Next, I could see preparations Emily and another man, the squaw's father perhaps, were making in some attempt at – *full* resurrection? That was certainly what it seemed like. My only points of reference to such were Christ's return to life after crucifixion, and those persons whom *he'd* resurrected during his life before that. Oh, and of course, *my own,* having my lifeblood drained dry, and being brought back afterward. I suppose I *did* know something of this after all.

Lastly, Emily spoke directly...

Come to me in the night as you can, dark angel. Go past the Tennessee
River, and I will meet you. Dream of me to speak of when you mean to journey,
and I'll receive it. I will be here for a while. As you've seen, I make preparations to
bring my cousin back entirely. It is a complicated spell, and will take time. I will
deal with my father later. This is **more** *important.*

Ahh, the girl suspected him already, or – picked it up when she'd looked into me, even though I'd held back in saying anything. Either way, she knew.

Should he return to the tavern and you choose to engage him further, find out
what you will – and deal with him as you wish. Again, I look forward to receiving
you as you can come, dear lady – Charissa.

Her former words, speaking so distantly of her father, triggered me awake instantly. I found myself reeling in their coldness. It was the same steely, calculated cold I'd blown across London in my ending of the Catholics I'd targeted. To feel it coming from another was chilling and sobering. Moreover, she was now roughly the same age I was just *before* my downward spiral. And she was coming into it already. I felt ever more drawn to her; though now, *protectiveness* – a mothering instinct even, was coming to the fore.

Her latter words to me, towards my going to her, warmed me more than I could say. Yet again solidifying how much I was growing to care for her. As such, her telling me to 'do with her father as I wished,' was now tilting towards the *opposite* of what I wanted to do with him only yesterday. I found myself hoping that later, when again I'd push drinks and allure the regulars, I'd see him return once more, and we would just *talk;* the way he had with the bartender before. Perhaps tomorrow or the next day I would 'dream of her' to tell Emily of my coming; but as for tonight, I would await her father for a second time.

• • • •

As I began my shift this dusk, I thought again of the father's return I'd hoped might repeat this night. Pondering this, my ability to compel people came to mind. But, from a distance? *Slim chance,* I thought. Still, young Emily was able to dream, even talk to me *within* one, from miles away. *Anything is possible,* I mused. So, for the duration of the fading day, I kept focused, thinking diligently of the father of Emily – coming here from his house.

Time passed while I busied myself with side work and idle chit-chat with the clientele. Just about as night had completely fallen, *he* arrived, both to my simultaneous expectation and surprise. Had the compelling from afar worked, or was it coincidence? I might never know, and it hardly mattered. What did was that he was here. Would he remember me? It would depend on whether his individual bent was blanking out during a stupor, or recall could be had.

"Hello again, miss," he began, ending the hanging question. "I believe it was you who helped me home last night, yes?"

So, a vague remembrance had he, asking for confirmation on my part to verify. Good enough. "It was I, yes sir," I replied, sitting down with him. "You overdid yourself last night, and I couldn't see you making it home without help. And now, it would seem, you're back for more this eve. If it's not too forward of me to ask, is there something at home perhaps – that prompts you to escape to here? You do not strike me as such a man who turns to drinking for escapism, especially since I've never seen you here before last night."

"You're astute, miss, I'll give you that," he began, "but you're only half right. Correct in that I don't make it a habit, nor am I 'regular' to this establishment. But, you're new here, am I right? I've been in

Clarksville for a long time with my family, and I actually *do* come in on occasion, yet in all that time, I have never seen – *you.* And I've never known anyone who works here to help a patron home – especially not a bar girl."

Hmmn! Already, the sober version of the man began to off-put with his suspiciousness and sense of entitlement. I was quickly concurring with the validity of Emily's issues with him.

"Well," I returned in rebuttal, "if you *aren't* here with much frequency as you say, you probably wouldn't know whether any staff helps a drunk home or not. But, from my short experience here, I would say you're likely right. As for me, fresh from London as I am, I simply saw you in need and responded. Which brings me back to my previous question. Having been to your home and meeting your wife and daughter, I'm still wondering if everything's all right – with yourself and them?"

"Not that it's any of your business, miss – ?"

"Charissa," I said in introduction.

"Robert," he returned, shaking my hand. "If you'd be so good as to do your job and get me a drink, perhaps I'll be forthcoming to your noisiness. Whiskey-sour, please."

Once more, his oh-so-charming nature made me want to rush him his drink – and throw it in his face! Instead, I served it politely, trying to get him to open up. To my bartender's chagrin, I poured myself a whiskey shot and downed it to build camaraderie with him. He considered me as I did – and proceeded to spill.

"No, ma'am, all is not well with the Mrs. and my girl. Yesterday, I crossed a line I cannot come back from, and though they know not

what it is, I fear it will soon unravel all around me. Already, Emily has left home once more to go join my brother and his damn Chickasaws. Kate is angry with me for what she believes to be my prior punishments upon Em being the very cause for her running away. She's not wrong, but it's far from the whole of it."

"What *is* 'the whole of it,' then?" I asked pointedly.

"Ha, ha," he chuckled with a smirk as though *knowing* he was being baited. "All I can say is that I've done something that will forever sever the already-strained relationship between my brother and I. I've taken something from him that I can never give back."

There it was. He'd basically told me *everything,* though simultaneously admitted to nothing. Very good, the predatory nature to perfection – something I knew just a little bit about. Had I not known the truth already, he'd have, in essence, given me nothing. As it was, he'd just corroborated all of it.

"What if – it could be given back?" I offered. Now *I* was going to have to dance around the truth just as much as he'd been throughout the conversation so far. "Not by *you,* mind you, but someone else, paying your penance *for* you, making the wrong you've done, right again? What would you say to that?"

"Ha, hah," he bellowed this time, nearly spitting out the whiskey he was about to swallow. "Woman, you speak in better riddles than myself! You have no idea what you're talking about. One *cannot* give back that which is gone for good. That which has *passed* – beyond."

He was getting closer to coming clean. That one was almost there. Another few drinks, which I proceeded to attend to, should about do the trick. But I wasn't entirely sure whether that's what I was still after.

I'd wanted to hear him *say* it, 'I took her life.' Then give him exacting justice for the act. But, I've rampaged down that bloody road already. Now I was with a *father* to someone I think I actually cared about. Helping her seek out the same style of vengeance I'd previously wrecked *wasn't* going to heal her, heal *them* – or restore their tattered bond. Re-venge wasn't the answer any longer. Re-demption was.

"Cat got your tongue, Charissa?" Robert asked, snapping me out of my muse. "You said something about someone 'paying my penance,' making my wrong right, or some damn-fool thing. I think you're talking out of your ass, but let's just pretend I'm interested. What in Sam hill do you mean?"

Ah ha, those next drinks *were* working! He was coming around. But, *what* could I tell him that wouldn't sound insane? We were, after all, speaking of a resurrection from the dead, though neither of us were about to admit to it. What could I say?

"Are you a Christian man, Robert?" I asked.

"Of course," he answered. "I go to great lengths to keep my family pure. Why?"

A Puritan then, perfect. "I know the phrase is not from specific scripture, sir, but do you believe that 'God works in mysterious ways' – or at least, *can?*"

"I do. But, what has that got to do with anything that we're talking about?"

"It has to do with a way in which your transgression might be righted – in a curious way. As we speak, there are preparations being made to circumvent – what you've done."

"You speak as though you would know anything about it. Yet, how *could* you possibly? What are you not telling me, woman?"

"I haven't been entirely forthright about the extent to which I've interacted with your daughter last night. While you were being put to bed, we talked to a degree. I learned then, that she would leave you this day, and go to your brother and the Chickasaws. ***God – "*** I fudged a bit, "brought me a dream that He would resurrect what you've 'stolen.'" I'd crossed the point of no return. We both knew what we were talking about now, and it was no longer likely that this would remain a civilized discussion. I would have to compel him the rest of the way to keep him from accusations of 'consorting with devils' and the like. For, I knew that's where this would end up in mere moments.

"The time shall come, I know not when, where all will be made ready to bring forth *the Indian's* return," I said flatly, starring into his eyes. "And *I will* be privy to it. I would endeavor to escort you there, to the place to whence it shall happen, and you might see God complete this work, and approve you of your guilt in the matter. But, you must agree to observe only, and *not* interfere. In accordance to this, do you accept my words and thereby, my invitation?"

"I do," he nodded, eyes glazed from both liquor and my assertions.

Chapter 26

Emily

Throughout the days to follow, Emily *did* keep Jed busy with her plan to combine the tribe's life celebration for Erika and her own revival spell to bring her back. She required both his and Tanyee's help in convincing the clan to adjust the ceremonial traditions to blend with the requirements of her intended enchantment. The biggest hurdle would be how they would prepare Erika's body for the next phase.

'Phase' was what it was all about; the moon's phases, specifically. What Emily proposed was, in essence, *reverse* lycanthropy. Since Erika's spirit was already moved into Nashoba, the goal was to spell-cast the wolf's state of being *into* that of the lunar cycle – pushing Nashoba *to become **human*** during the phases of the full moon. To wit, an 'inverse werewolf,' where Erika herself might manifest during the days and nights of the full cycle. No small task.

By the specifics of the grimoires, and combined with the 'spirit-animal bonding' already cast, the key physical element needed was the *ashes* of the deceased. Erika's body would need to cremated, and that remaining dust lathered *into* the wolf's fur, where her spirit now abided. It was not completely unheard of that Indians would burn their dead, but it *was* rare – and *not* the Chickasaw way. Where these traditions occasionally occurred were more toward tribes of the Georgia region, the Choctaw or Cherokee perhaps.

Thus, adjustments would need to be made, and accepted methods let go. To which, when Emily sat down with the couple to explain, uncertainty prevailed.

"Em," Tanyee began, "I cannot say how the chiefs will react to that which you propose. It is true that certain tribes have, at times, been known to burn the body, but they aren't of this region, and certainly not the way of we Chickasaws. I myself do not know how I feel about that – your calling for Erika's body to be put to the fire," she concluded, her breath hitching.

"What about," Jed began, "if we made clear to them that Erika resides now within Nashoba?"

"Yes," concurred Emily, "and that, combined with my applied magics, we *can* restore her to her former self?"

"Perhaps," Tanyee returned, "but, as far as you've explained, it would only be during the full moon where she would be herself again, yes? That may not be enough for the elders."

"It would be better than nothing, would it not?" questioned Em.

"If there were a way," Tanyee continued, "to show them, beyond all shadow of doubt, that my daughter *is* now one with our wolf, they might be swayed. The question is, how would we do that?"

Emily puzzled for a moment to this, then came to an answer. "Tanyee, show me, in detail, *all* elements of the burial tradition and ceremony. If you walk me through it, I might glean a proper place within it, to cast a spell to reveal to *all* what only we three know to be true. If it can be shown clear, do you think they would yield to the break of tradition?"

"Yes, there is a good chance – *if* you can."

"Then let my lessons begin."

• • • •

The day had come – the time to lay Erika to rest. By tradition, it was to be *under* the house, or chickee, where the deceased had resided. Tanyee had sought out the chiefs to explain to them their unique circumstances with regard to their daughter – and the wolf. They were neither accepting nor rejecting of the requested deviation from the norm. They took a 'show us' attitude, granting also that she not be 'sealed away' immediately into the ground.

Erika was placed into position within her plot with her head facing east, where a fire was lighted and *hung* a distance over it. Normally, the person was *fully* interred at this point, so the fire would burn on the ground *above* the body at the head. Due to the leeway they'd been given, this alteration had been allowed. Four nights was the duration of the custom, which was to keep away bad spirits. Ultimately, the goal was that they would soon see *her* spirit – in Nashoba, who remained by the gravesite, close to the fire.

It was during this period that Emily set into effect her 'vision' spell. An invocation for the eyes of the 'grave watchers' to be opened and see Erika's spirit aura over Nashoba. Em remained there over the course of those days, never leaving the wolf, never ceasing her chants. Fasting was the way of the people who watched, and Em adopted the practice herself in homage to those who would consider her prospectus of the 'resurrection.' Jed and Tanyee were appreciative and touched by her dedication to her cousin and her craft, bringing her water and support when she needed it.

At last came the morning of the fourth day, and just before daybreak, *all* the people, both old and young, went to plunge four times in water. Upon completion of this ritual, the soul of the dead was purported to be 'satisfied' to 'go up.' Following this, all the assemblage gathered to Jed and Tanyee's home, where the principal chief would speak his piece for Erika's ascension.

To this he said, "Our oshetik, Erika, whom we have prepared in these days to pass onward – *has not*. Cannot. For, she has come to be with her Choctaw, Nashoba. We have kept watch as the fire has burned, and have seen her within him, intertwined there in her spirit animal. She has been captured there, through the spell cast from before, by Jed's niece. Now, it is by *her* hand that Erika may rise again. And, whether by wisdom or folly, it is *only* she who can move her along. So, it is by this recognition that I hereby appoint Emily – as *the guardian*. She may take Erika and go to the hill in the open country – and continue *the fire* as she sees fit. She will take the ripe corn and ripe beans, to make our oshetik ripened also. It is spoken."

And so it was. She had spell-cast, and they had seen. It was to her the honor had been passed to complete what she'd set forth to do. She bowed to the chief, then to her uncle and his wife, and in humility seated herself there amongst the people, next to the hole where her cousin lay.

· · · ·

By mid-morning Emily was exhausted. Jed led her to the accommodations they'd made for her to lay her down.

"You did well, niece," Jed complimented, brushing her hair back as she laid down her head.

"I did all right, I suppose," replied Emily. "I dozed off a number of times – those were a long four days! Charissa came to me in daydreams when I napped."

"You don't say? What of that?"

"She was ready to come and see me here, as I'd offered her to, in these days; or *nights* that is, in her case. Since we were in the period of burial, I prompted that she wait till later as I couldn't get away until after. I will dream to her as I sleep now, perhaps that she come upon the eve I enact the final spell. The full moon is only a day away, after all."

"That worked out well, yes," agreed Jed. "Rest now, sweet Em, dream to your friend, however it is that you do that, and be still." He knelt over, kissed her forehead and left her to it.

Chapter 27

Charissa

In the scope of things, it had come to pass. I'd forced upon myself exodus from London because of my bloodlust and recklessness. I'd come here to the new world and needed to create distractions to buffer against how lost I truly felt. Now I had them; an Indian wolf-girl, cousin to a young witch, and her maniacal Puritan hunter-father. And within only a few short days I'd managed to wedge myself into a pickle within their whole drama. Emily seemed entirely comfortable leaving her father to my methods of 'dealing' with injustices. Now I was poised to do nearly the opposite of those intentions: Bring him *with* me to observe whatever sorcery she'd be attempting in her bid to bring her cousin back. There were so many ways by this could go wrong, it was ridiculous. I didn't know the half of it; the road to hell was always paved with good intentions.

Still, I set forth this night toward the Tennessee River to my rendezvous with Emily, my 'invitee' lingering behind me at a safe distance, 'in tow.' When Em had dreamt again to me the day following my talk with Robert, she'd said all would be ready, and that she wanted me there. Would she want her father? I doubted it. Would I have even considered the idea were it not for my ability to compel? Absolutely not! This was the only way to 'manage' such a man as he. At a reasonable distance behind, just to watch – and see the restoration of the girl's life he had taken – to give him a sense of resolution, and perhaps the beginnings of a mending with his daughter. Probably not at all what Emily had in mind just now, and certainly not how she'd anticipated *I* would deal with the matter. But, having the advantage of hindsight, already knowing the horrible consequences of a path hellbent on vengeance, I'd decided to take the higher road. I hadn't, and wouldn't, tell her of his unseen presence in the background; plus I had complete confidence now in the strength of my asserted will upon another. He would stay back, and see only what I wanted him to. Not Emily's witchcraft, and not her within the Indian lands; *just* the resurrection of the girl. That was the plan at least. I'd no way of knowing then that, even as I led ahead of him, *another **followed,*** to his rear. *My* other.

. . . .

I approached the little witch in like fashion to the first time I'd ever seen her – from a good distance away across the plain. Unlike that time, however, we strode *to* each another, rather than my watching her recede into her home, while she'd been unaware I was even present. Although we didn't run *to* one another, our paces increased as we advanced. We greeted with clasped hands and a bit of a side-hug, this being only our second actual meeting.

"I'm so glad you were able to come, Charissa," began Emily. "I had planned to see you again sooner, but I had the four days of burial preparations to contend with – and work my magic for the elders to grant me *guardianship* of Erika's body, which we burned at dusk atop the hill the chief sent us to, her father and I, my uncle."

"That must have been hard for him, I'd imagine," I said, not fully grasping exactly why she'd done this. "The cremation has something to do with your resurrection spell, I take it?"

"*Everything* to do with it, my friend," she replied as she began escorting me back from whence she'd come. As we walked, she continued, "I'm casting a werewolf spell basically, but in reverse. Since we *already **have*** a wolf, and Erika's inside of him, the spell-cast tying Nashoba to the lunar cycle *should* turn him to a human female during the course of the full moon, instead of the other way around. The spell necessitates that her dissolved ashes be lathered into his coat, completing the physical requirements of their union."

"I see," I said, my hackles raising a bit at the mention of *werewolf.* I didn't know much about lycans, and I was only now learning about being a vampire; but something in my memory concerning the lore of both told me that the two were not a good mix together. And presumably, we were walking headlong towards my meeting the wolf. I hadn't the foresight before coming that this was specifically Emily's intention in the matter. I bit my lip, however, continuing on with her as though everything were fine. I glanced once or twice to my rear as we proceeded, to see that Robert was still in trail further behind. He was, perfect. A Christian zealot to the rear and a wolf further on ahead – what could be better? What could possibly go wrong here?

"Again, I'm sorry," Emily interjected as we strolled, pulling me out of my sudden anxiety. "I know you'd been ready to come see me sooner, days ago. But between the groundwork I've had to do for this

and your needs to only come at night, well, it couldn't be helped."

"Not at all," I said. "It's perfectly fine, and I understand completely. I simply count myself as fortunate to have met someone else that is, shall we say, a 'supernatural' like myself." And very soon, I would likely meet another.

• • • •

Jed sat upon the hill where the fire which had consumed Erika's mortal shell still burned. The licks of flame danced eerily against the brightness of the full moon's light. He was cozied up with Nashoba almost in the same manner that he might have with his daughter in a similar setting. To him, of course, that's exactly what he was doing. He could feel Erika's same warmth and aura as if they'd never missed a beat, and indeed, they hadn't. He surmised he would have never made it through being present for this cremation had he not known she *was* still here.

Earlier, prior to Emily's setting out to meet Charissa, they had gone to a nearby spring to gather from it; pure and natural water as the spell called for, to blend into a more liquid form, Erika's ashes, to be absorbed *into* the wolf. This same wolf who now stirred to the approach of the returning Emily – and an unknown. At that point, it was all instinct, *all* Nashoba who came to the fore, bolting from Jed, taking off into the distance where a scent *other* than just Em's emanated powerfully – and had to be dealt with.

• • • •

It all happened very quickly as we'd clearly entered the perimeter of the wolf's senses. With *my* equivalent sense of sight and smell, I became aware of his sprint toward me much quicker than Emily, but it still wasn't quite fast enough. She yelped an emphatic *No!* as the beast careened into me, sending both of us sailing backward from Em. I basically let myself take the impact as I'd already anticipated this meeting with trepidation. I just wanted to get it over with. We tumbled and rolled, the wolf growling wildly, slashing its jaws at me; while I, in turn, barred my own formidable fangs at him. It all must have been quite a sight to behold as Em went from trying to call him off to being mesmerized at the ensuing battle. I moved and darted, matching all of his animal-like speed and agility in our little dance. Unlike this 'Nashoba,' I was keeping in mind that I grappled with not only a beast, but the *cousin* within. I wondered though, *where was **she** now?*

Emily must have mirrored my thought as she snapped out of it, screaming "Erika! Enough," whipping her hands about in some kind of casting. A kind of barrier or gust of some sort then came between me and the wolf I wrestled with, breaking us suddenly apart. Our bout broken up, Em inserted herself between us, again with a "Nash, *no!* She's a friend. Stop now, boy!" Then, turning to me, she continued, *"What* are you, Charissa? You spoke simply of a curse you had, but this!"

"You wondered before," I began, getting up, "about 'the dark' you sensed in me? *Why* you had confidence in me to deal concisely with your father? *This* is why. Emily, you are a witch. I – am a vampire."

"Can't go out in the day, of course!" exclaimed Emily in reply. "It makes perfect sense now. But, were you ever going to tell me?"

"Perhaps – perhaps not. I'm uncertain actually as to my intentions whether to tell you or no. But, as we came here speaking of your wolf, I began anticipating that it might react to me in this way. One predator can sniff out another quite easily. Given that, I concluded it better to let it happen and just get it over with. Now the proverbial 'elephant is out of the room,' at least."

"Perhaps 'on its *way* out,' more like," was Emily's response. Now that what I am was coming clear to her, her *core* familial ties were kicking in somewhat, as I'd hoped. Her brain doing the progressive math having seen me in 'animal action,' she pointedly asked, "You – haven't hurt my father, have you? I know I said 'do as you will with him,' but that was before I knew – *this."*

"Oh, come now, Emily. You sensed something sinister in me from the start, and you banked on it as adequate to mete out whatever Robert had coming. *Now* that you've seen the true beast within, you backpedal. But, not to worry, I'm glad to see some concern on your part come forth. I have not harmed him in any way. I've done little more than compel him a bit."

"Compel him to do what?" she asked.

"Just *talk* with me, dear, nothing else. I'll tell you more later. For now, should you not get on with the spell? *I* would very much like to bring Erika to the fore, over the wolf, given our little skirmish just now. I don't know that Nashoba likes me much."

Emily laughed, "Yes, ha hah, of course," getting her head back in the game. And I, for one needed it there and *off* the subject of Robert, still far enough away, but present nonetheless; a detail I *absolutely* didn't want to reveal. Her confidence in me had already waned a tad learning I'm a vampire; finding out I'd brought her idiot father to witness, even

at a distance, could create a serious problem between us, and I didn't want that. That's on me, of course, as I'm the fool who brought him in the first place. One thing was certainly clear: whether operating as a vengeful murderess, or looking out for another's best interests, I clearly made questionable choices either way. Well, I've said it before, c'est la vie. The die was cast, and so too, soon would be *the spell.*

· · · ·

I hung back behind Jed the uncle, father of the fallen Erika, at the foot of the little hill they'd chosen for the ritual. Emily was at the top warming up her chant with Nashoba, or 'Nasherka,' as Jed called it, next to her.

"My word is done, by rising moon and setting sun," she began.

She continued to recite it till it became a mantra. After a short time of this, she turned to Jed where he held out the urn with the girl's ashes. Next, she nodded for me to produce the flask of pure spring water collected earlier which she'd given me to hold. I rose up moving parallel to Jed and presented it. As we stood next to each other holding the elements, she herself removed a small red vial from her breast pocket. Red like blood – easily garnering my direct attention.

She nodded again to the question she read in my eyes, *was it a sample of Erika's blood?* Yes. She must've drained some from her corpse before they'd burned it, I presumed. She gestured at me to exchange the flask for the vial with her.

"It is only fitting, *vampire,*" she began, "that *you* should hold the blood."

Ah, she *did* have a flair for the apropos! I knew I liked this girl. The hand-off completed, she began pouring the water into the urn she'd blinked at Jed to open. She gently poured while intermittently mixing the concoction together with her free hand. She continued this for only as long as it took for its texture to become the consistency of a thin paint, and no more. Having reached the level she wished, she blinked to me to pour out the vial. We grinned slightly to one another at this, both of us noting the irony. It did not escape my notice either, that we seemed to be mirroring the Communion sacrament in some morbidly ironic fashion.

With all the elements now brought together, she removed her stirring hands from the urn, thick with the stuff, and turned back around to Nashoba. She reached out to him and began lathering the mixture into his coat.

Chapter 28
'Erika'

Then Emily recited, *"Spirit of the wolf, you who wanders the wild lands, you who stalks in silent shadows, you who runs and leaps between the moss-covered trees, lend me your primal strength and the wisdom of your glowing eyes. Teach me to relentlessly track my desires and to stand in defense of those I love. Show me the hidden paths and the moonlit fields. Fierce spirit, walk with me in my solitude, howl with me in my joy and guard me as I move through this world.*
    My word is done, by rising moon and setting sun."

Nashoba was fully soaked with the mixture now. Emily rubbed his neck affectionately, then backed off her hands from him, beginning to move them in magical gestures. She picked up a stick and put it to the fire; once lit, she shifted it gently back and forth in the air in specific motions. Nashoba started a low, moaning howl while stretching out both his front and hind legs. They began shaking – the metamorphosis had commenced.

She continued her recital, *"I am the wolf. I am the spirit of the wilderness. I am the shadow in the woods. If you walk in the untouched forests like me, I will sing for you. I will talk to you with a voice only those who love me and nature are able to hear. Do not fear me.*
    My word is done, by rising moon and setting sun."

The limbs weren't just shaking now, but convulsing; indeed, the entire body. It was no longer wolf, but neither was it fully human yet either. Tail and snout had diminished, front legs were becoming arms, hair on the head grew longer. The howl was changing in pitch into a girl's cry.

"A warrior's strength is measured by the size of her heart. She is respectfully humble. She will stand with honor. She will fight with love. In the face of adversity and for the ones she loves, she will be a voice and a shield. She will be a beacon to light the way home for the old. She will gently make way for the young. She is a sister, daughter – she is a warrior.
    My word is done, by rising moon and setting sun."

These were the words for Erika, to bring her forth completely. The former had been for Nashoba, to *start* the transition from wolf. And yet, the process seemed to have slowed, perhaps even stopped somehow. The body had fully formed from a four-legged to two-legged being, a full coat of fur had diminished to heavy hair, skin not yet showing through. The face of a female was distinguishable, and her jawline showed razor sharp human teeth over canine fangs. Paws had become claw-like hands and feet, breasts had grown. But, suddenly, it all seemed to come to a halt right there.

Seeing something was clearly amiss, Emily burned into another recital with fervor, trying desperately to coax the remainder of the transformation, *"I give you this one thought to keep – I am with you still – I do not sleep. I am a thousand winds that blow, I am the diamond glints on*

snow, I am the sunlight on ripened grain, I am the gentle autumn rain. When you awakened in the morning's hush, I am the swift, uplifting rush of quiet birds in circled flight. I am the soft stars that shine at night. Do not think of me as gone – I am with you still – in each new dawn.

My word is done, by rising moon and setting sun."

The moon had been risen for a good while now, but it appeared that the sun had surely set on the spell that was to have brought Erika completely back. She was – stuck – in between. She had become, in essence, what legends call *a werewolf.*

"No!" Emily cried, shaken to her core that the spell had stalled. She'd put everything into this. She stood agape at 'Erika' before her, *she* equally reeling at what was happening. Em turned back to Charissa and Jed still behind her, in dismay and guilt. Jed was too much in shock to offer much by way of support, but the vampire reached out and squeezed her arm.

Erika reached out to Em's other arm then, but gently, knowing a firmer grip having these claws might not be wise. Spinning back around, Emily looked headlong into her cousin's pleading eyes. Pleading, because she was trying to speak, but no voice besides growls and grunts were coming out. She looked at Em ever stronger, tightening her grip on her ever-so-slightly. Erika was trying to get focused beyond this struggle to talk, and attempt to get into Em's mind instead.

"Cousin, she said in her thoughts, *"it's all right. This **isn't** what you intended I know, but I have been one with Nash for some time now, and I love him. I am **not** revolted and this isn't terrible. It's just hard to talk!"*

Emily heard her in her head just fine, and leaned over laughing a

little that not talking was the only thing really bothering her. "All right," she began in answer aloud, "but I'm not going to stop trying. You're tied to the full moon cycle, *just like* a werewolf now, so you'll still return to 'Nashoba-wolf' form at the end of it. So, it's only right that you ought to be able to be *completely* human during full phase. I will *not* give up, my cousin."

Erika smiled back in a 'wolfish' grin, squeezing Em's hand in her big claw palm.

. . . .

Further away from them all, in the distance, a voice came to Robert in similar fashion as Em and Erika's exchange, as he observed all of this from his little dugout.

"Silly man," the voice said, *"you've been duped: It is not **God** by whose power this supposed resurrection has been given – no, quite the opposite. You see? Charissa lied to you. God would have restored the girl fully, but the black magic of the Dark One can only bring her back as far as a beast – a demon. And look, it is all by your own daughter's hand. You may love her, but it's your duty to take care of her transgressions,"* a female voice whispered in his ear.

"Why would she have lied about it?" he said aloud, fixating suddenly on Charissa there in the distance. He *had* seen her do her part in the ritual; she was as much involved as the rest of them – even his turncoat brother, right there with the group too. What could be the purpose in bringing him out here to see it all, if it *hadn't* been a restoration ordained by God, as Charissa had said? Only one reason he could think of: Lure him away out of his territory – to kill him for *his*

transgression in their own camp!

As if sensing his very thoughts, the woman's voice continued, *"Yess, of course they mean to kill you, dragging your miserable hide way out here! You thought Charissa meant you well? Would lead you to your redemption? That she'd*

befriended you? Yes, I once thought that as well. But, she's a demon, just like that
wolf-thing there, and your witch offspring too.

You're the only one privy to what's gone on here, and the only one who can
protect your community from the havoc their combined might could wreak. But
presently, you must retreat straightaway! If you stay to try and stop them by
*yourself, you **will** fall. Go, I will cover you, should one or all pursue."*

Her voice was soft but firm, and English, like Charissa's. She moved from
him like a shadow, stealthily to his fore, to block any advancement from
members of the group they'd watched, should it come. Regrettably, Robert's
retreat was not as fluid, creating a rustle that any wolf or a vampire, even at a
distance, could detect.

. . . .

Erika and Charissa heard it immediately. Movement from deeper in the woods
surrounding them. Erika's (and Nash's) senses and memories picked up on
the familiar scent of Robert, somewhere about. Charissa's own ultra-awareness
smelled not only his, but – another's. Someone she *knew. It couldn't be,* she
thought.

There was no more time for contemplating it though, as Erika the wolf-girl
bolted from the group, her recollection of her death and Nash's bad vibes
towards Robert taking over. Charissa took off after her, knowing this could go
all kinds of wrong. *She **had,*** stupidly in retrospect, brought Robert here – and
if whom she imagined were

present also, *that* was on her too. She caught up to Erika quickly, and
engaged to stop her progress. "No, Erika!" commanded Charissa. "We *both*
know who's out there, but *I'm* responsible for him being here! I should've
known better; I wanted him to see you become *you* again – but not this. I didn't
imagine the spell would fail, and he *wouldn't* see the girl he killed *not* come
back to life. I'm sorry, but you have to let me deal with this. Besides, he's with
someone else, I think – whom I'm also accountable for. Please, stay. I've got
this," she finished, still with her hand planted to Erika's chest, holding her back.
She eased up and Erika remained still, no longer attempting to advance. "Thank
you," Charissa said in parting, and took off into the night.

It didn't take long for Emily to trail after Charissa and Erika. Jed followed too, but in a slow, zombie-like pace, still half in shock. When Emily reached Erika, she found her surprisingly still and stationary, as Charissa had asked. Em came to her immediately, touching her face and looking into her yellow wolf eyes, to expedite their mental communication. "What's happened?" she began. "You took off, then Charissa after you. I know you both heard a disturbance nearby, but now you're here alone and she is gone. What? – "

*"Your vampire friend, whoever she is, says the intruders are **her** responsibility. One of them is your father – she says she brought him here to see me return to life – I know not why – to absolve him perhaps. But, if that's true, he **never saw me,** only a beast. So, all good intentions of your 'Charissa' are now for naught. Where did she come from, this 'vampiress' of yours?"*

"Long story, my cousin. We met when she, as a helpful barmaid at the tavern, brought Father home drunk, where I assume he'd been

commiserating what he'd done to you. We'd chatted in the doorway while Mother put him to bed, and had an immediate repour. I'd invited her here through dream-walks, much like you and I have done throughout our lives. I hadn't known she was a vampire prior to when you and Nash attacked her earlier, but I sensed she had a knack for sharp justice, and thought she might deal with Father ideally. Bringing him here secretly to see all of this was the last thing I would've expected."

*"And not good for **any** of us, either. Still, it seems she meant well."* She turned to see her father finally approaching. *"Would you remain here with Inki please, Em? I may have agreed to Charissa's request to stay behind and let her deal with the 'spies,' but my instincts tell me I should move along and go check on her."*

"Not that she deserves it, given her lack of better judgement with my Father, but yes, go ahead. I'll stay with Uncle Jed, try to help him through this. Like Charissa taking ownership for her bad choices, I must confess to him that it's my fault the spell didn't restore you wholly."

Erika growled affirmatively, hugged her cousin, and loped off after their vampire.

Chapter 29
Charissa

The scent of Robert was fading fast, but *hers* was ever present – it was close. She had to be nearby, waiting for me. But how had she attached herself to him? How had she even found him? How could she know any of this? Answers would come soon enough as I saw a figure up ahead in a clearing beyond the tree line. She was no longer in retreat, but clearly lingering for my approach. I slowed my pace as the pursuit was all but done. I neared, and sure enough, the truth my sense of smell had battled my logic over was proved by my sense of sight. It *was **her.***

Andrea.

"How in heaven or hell do you come to be here?" I demanded. "And why were you with that man?"

"What man?" she giggled. "I see no *man* here," she cackled. "And why am I here, you ask? To be closer to you again, my maker! To you *and* the things you've connected yourself to! What could be better? After all, you took *away* he whom I'd been attached to, so it's only equal balance that I should dabble with those you've now fastened to!"

"But – the long journey overseas," I began, "the trip here, to Tennessee of all places?"

"Same ship as you, darling. Certainly big enough for you not to detect me. Different wagons to get *here*, of course. Don't think you'd miss me if I'd been in the same one as you there! And my, my – lovely, little Clarksville! And the Laydons! What an interesting, quaint family drama they are! I must say, you've gotten yourself all bundled up with them nicely, haven't you? I have to admit, I'm rather unclear as to the specifics of the wolf, and why they were trying to draw a dead Indian girl out of it. One who I believe our dear Mr. Laydon shot? Rash, by the way, bringing him out here to relieve his guilt in the hopes of seeing her come back to life by some backwards werewolf spell. Nice imagination on the little witch's part though. But, trying to convince him of a 'God-blessed' resurrection? Really, Charissa! Well, I've made sure he's rejected

125

that idea – not that I needed much help considering her ridiculous spell has produced nothing but a beast!"

"Are you quite finished, Andrea? Perhaps you'd like to meet 'the beast'? I'm sure she'd enjoy tearing you limb from limb – as would I."

"Then why didn't you do it in the first place, Charissa? Why not simply have killed me and been done with it – like James? But no, you decided to make me like yourself instead!"

"I thought it was a good fit for you. It seemed to me like your character would be well-suited for this."

"Did you now? Well, your 'thinking,' or lack thereof, seems to be a re-occurring pattern, doesn't it? Not sleeping with James when he was

yours, murdering him and all those priests, even your woebegone effort to redeem the witch's idiot father by bringing him all the way here! Oh, and let's not forget your masterpiece – turning me. It's a wonder you've made it this far on your journey in one piece. Time to rectify that, 'I think.'"

That said, she was upon me like flies to dung. It wasn't that I was unprepared for the attack, but my brain was admittedly still reeling to the implausibility of her being here. She was clearly still in the early throes of vampirism; all hunger and vengeance, just as I had been initially. I was relating very much to Nashoba the wolf just now; basic, raw animal instincts to begin with, then domesticated by becoming bonded to the Indian girl and her human 'pack.'

I was going to have to *relate* to this battle quickly though, and get my own self back into visceral-mode to compete with my progeny. Her first move had her plowing into me like a cannonball, sending both of us off our feet. From a hard landing, I rolled, using our combined momentum to flip her off of me. She landed face first in the dirt, and I was right back on top of her before she could regroup, pushing her head further into the soft ground, poised upon her backside. Countering this, she dug her feet and lower limbs in, pulling her head and neck out from under me. She reared straight up then, throwing me off just as I had her moments ago.

I landed on my back, and now it was she quickly back on top of me, hands going straight for my throat. Then she moved those hands to holding my head by the cheeks while she planted her nose into my neckline, taking in a good whiff. She rolled her nose as far as my chin, then turned it up so her mouth came around and neared my lips. This

was painfully familiar.

"Remember when we were like this, Charissa?" she recollected.

Oh, I did, and I didn't like it one bit. I recoiled, attempting to head-butt her off, but she reacted quicker and butted me back in the forehead with her own, driving my head into the ground as I'd done to her a few seconds ago. The kid-gloves were off now, no longer playing around with trying to kiss me. Fangs out, she bore down into my neck, penetrating deeply. First she was just feeding, taking a good long swig of me; but then I felt her tense – she was about to pull away – and rip my throat out. Suddenly, her eyes sprang open in surprise, along with her mouth agape, before she had a chance to complete a critical, tearing bite! The next thing I knew, she'd been yanked off me hard, and tossed asunder.

The wolf – Erika.

My eyes were as wide as Andrea's had been, then blinking to realize *what* had actually just happened. I was getting to my feet, musing as to the irony of my earlier words of *the 'beast' enjoying tearing her limb-from-limb*. It was coming to pass. Ripping and tearing at her Erika was, with no end in sight. Andrea had been ready for me – but not for this. I had to intervene, and keep Erika from becoming a murderer, not that Andrea didn't have this coming. But better me than she.

"Erika, stop!" I shouted, barreling into her to break it up. "This isn't you! Or at least, it wasn't supposed to be, if the spell had worked right. Either way, I don't want blood on your hands for my mess!"

She grappled with me for a moment, half of her wanting to get back to viscerating Andrea. "No," I continued, "you don't want to do this. *I'm* the one with blood on my hands already, and regardless, I'm the one responsible for turning her into this – *my* mistake. You don't need to take yourself to this place, though I much appreciate your help."

She eased up from pushing against me, grunting a muffled reply, indicating, I think, that she understood. I could tell she wanted to speak, but her stalled metamorphosis between wolf and human had brought her up short of verbal communication. I turned to go back to dealing with Andrea – but she was already gone. She must have deduced the odds of coming out ahead between the both of us weren't much in her favor, and bolted during the distraction.

Erika's instincts, just as mine, were to once again give chase; and once more I held her back, saying, "No, I've got this." But, before I started off, the voice of another spoke, shouting out, "Wait! Don't go yet, I want to talk to *you*."

Emily.

Jed was with her too, naturally, but hung back to let we three supernaturals have our huddle. "Just let her go for now, please," Emily continued, coming up to us. "You can explain to me all about her as we go back to Clarksville, you and I. I need to return and deal with my father properly, as I thought *you* were going to – but clearly didn't."

"Emily, I – " I tried to say, but was stopped short.

She went on, stepping over my words, "Nevermind, Charissa. I don't care. Erika seems to think you meant well in bringing Father with you tonight, so I'll give you the benefit of the doubt to that. But it still put

all of us in a precarious position by doing so. Do you have any idea how many years I've spent coming into these very woods trying to *distance* myself from him, keeping him *away* from here while I sought out my cousin? And your first thought was to bring him with you! And for all I know, *his* presence could've been the element contributing to the spell going wrong. The attendance of one diametrically *opposed* to the practice could've tainted the atmosphere we were attempting to create, I don't know. All I'm saying is, his being here did nothing to help; even though you must've been thinking to *help him* somehow, to see Erika's return to life, I'm guessing?"

"Yes, that's it exactly!" I said, getting a word of defense in where I could. "I hoped it would be the beginning of a mending between the two of you as well. I know you anticipated I would deal with him in quite an opposite fashion, but believe me, I've spent the last several years of my life literally *attacking* things in that manner, and it's a dark and dangerous road. I wanted better for you and yours."

Once more, she found the truth and sincerity in my words that she seemed to have a knack for finding. She bowed her head to me in acknowledgment of my good intentions, easing up in her rising anger towards me. I then bowed my head to her as well, taking her hands in mine to say, "I'm sorry."

"I know you are," she said, "and if you want to make it up to me, come with me back to town, and we'll deal with things as we must, though perhaps not as we'd *like*. And do it, together."

"Done and done," I replied.

Erika grunted and growled.

Chapter 30
Emily

Emily and Charissa took their time on the way back. It was decided best to leave Erika behind, being stuck in her 'werewolf' state, even if she did revert back to Nash's normal form at dawn. Neither appearance of wolf or Indian girl would do anything but draw hate and fear from those in Clarksville. The witch and the vampire talked much on the journey, but Charissa kept ever alert to the possible reappearance of Andrea. It *was* one of the main reasons for going back...

"So, you think she's going to continue duping my father through her ability to compel?" asked Emily. "And you can do that too. It's how *you* got Father to come with you, yes?"

"Yes, and yes," Charissa returned. "From what she said, she intends to toy with me by using those I've become associated with as her puppets; ergo, you and your family. She does this because I took *away* her lover from her, my former fiancée."

"Just a moment, *what?*" Emily queried, dismayed. "Your beau left you for Andrea, you're saying? And later, after you were turned, you went back, killed him, and *turned* her also. Why not just slay her too, and be done with them both?"

"Believe me, I'm asking myself that quite a lot at the moment. It has certainly turned about and is biting me in the bum. At the time, I fancied it a cruel sense of justice for her. You see, we'd been friends, she and I. She was much different than me, quite liberal as opposed to my more conservative sense. For some reason, I felt being this bizarre sort of creature suited her character very well. Thus, rather than just a quick death, she could deal with being this instead, and probably relish it. I was right – more than I could've dreamed. Because it's now a dream turned nightmare."

"Yes, *yours,* which has now trickled down to me as well. What do you think she'll do next?"

"It depends. She seemed to have discovered much with regard to our circumstances; I'd wager she's been observing us closely for a while. Curse me for not having sensed her sooner. I should have!"

"Perhaps she compelled *you* not to detect her?"

"Smart girl. That makes sense. Anyway, her next move might be along the lines of compelling Robert to rally the town for a witch or werewolf hunt. Something like that I'd guess, *if* she escalates."

"You've given me no reason to think she wouldn't, Charissa." Em paused momentarily, contemplating that. Then she suddenly gasped, "Oh my goodness! What if she's figured out about my mother being a witch also!"

Charissa replied, "I can't think of any interaction we've had, you and I, where your mum's hand was tipped to have revealed that."

"It doesn't matter," Em came back, "because *you* sensed my magic

before you even met me! If you could, as a vampire, then she'd be able to as well. Oh no. That's the first thing she'll do, try to turn Father against Mom, maybe try to hurt her, and use that to threaten us!"

"Easy, Emily. You're jumping to conclusions and scaring yourself. I'm not saying you're wrong, but Andrea *hadn't* figured out all about Erika and what we were trying to do with that spell, so there's no reason to think she has a clue about your mum. Still, since it's occurred to you, and it *is* plausible, neither would I rule it out."

"Oh God," Emily concluded.

"*Speaking* of **him**, my dear," Charissa began, moving onto an entirely separate thought, "It's crossed *my* mind that perhaps the element of 'God the Son' might be incorporated into the spell to return Erika to form."

"Whatever do you mean?" stammered Emily, caught completely off-guard. "I'm not following."

"Consider this: I utilized the notion of the restorative powers of Christ to compel Robert to come and see Erika 'resurrect.' Em, what *if* – *that's* the necessary element to turn her back to human completely? Christ returned from the dead. *I am* a resurrected creature, albeit darkly. And, believe it or not, I used to dutifully serve the Lord. Though it is true I no longer reflect it well, it *was* a missions' trip that actually led to this dreadful existence. What if, in the spirit of Christ's return, *and* the addition of *my* vampiric blood to the spell, we could complete it fully? What do you think? Does that make any sense to you, young witch?"

"It's not an utterly awful idea – at all! I rather like it, actually. In all the time I've been growing in the craft, I've been trying to balance my

faith in God with what I've been learning – and have come up short. I adore Jesus, but the manner in which Father represents His ways almost makes me want to renounce Him."

"It's the last thing I'd wish for you to do, Em, but I'd renounce your father long before I'd renounce the Lord."

"I'm just about ready to do that regardless, Chris. And thank you for the idea on the spell. I imagine that, depending upon its success, we'll find out if the Lord blesses or curses *the craft*."

"Indeed, my dear."

* * * *

The events of the evening combined with the good deal of time it took getting back to Clarksville meant the nighttime hours were running short for Charissa. Beginning to realize this, she asked Emily if she'd mind overmuch being carried. For, it was time to bring out her vampire speed for the remainder of the miles; which, if Em was left to her own, she'd never keep up. Emily accepted, and received the 'ride' of her life once Charissa got going.

They'd closed the gap of the remaining distance in short order, arriving to the outskirts of Clarksville well within the hour. Coming to a halt, Charissa set Emily back down on her own two feet. It took Em a moment to regain her composure in the wake of such an adrenaline rush. "Gracious me!" she said, catching her breath. "That was incredible! So, you can run fast, compel people to do as you wish, what else?"

"Superior strength, agility, and heightened senses," replied Charissa. "And in order to 'earn' these advantages, all I have to do is stay inside

during the day – and, oh, just drink people's blood to remain alive. That's all. I guess I'm lucky that I don't have to literally *consume* people by eating them, as my cannibal maker would have."

"That's terrible," said Em. "I'm sorry."

"Don't be. Those responsible for sending us to the isle of those beasts have paid the price. I made sure of that. Unfortunately, I also made the mistake of 'making' Andrea during that same period, which *I'm sorry,* has wound up being blow-back into your life. I could never have imagined her stalking me across an ocean and winding up here in Tennessee as well."

"Ironic how we don't have the foresight to see what's ahead, even as 'supernaturals,'" Emily offered. "Meanwhile, what shall we do next, m'lady? You're about out of time before dawn is here, and I don't know that I wish to return home alone, not knowing what to expect." After a millisecond, it came to her, "I know! I could put you in the basement!"

"Perfect – unless that turns out to be where Andrea's holed up as well," Charissa half-chuckled. "If it *is,* this time I'll rectify my mistake of turning her, once and for all."

And for the second time in as many minutes, Emily said, "Gracious!"

· · · ·

A short while later, as the first hues of the night sky began to shift towards the dawn, Emily and Charissa skulked about the Laydon residence, strategizing their entry during this early hour. Should, God forbid, Robert be present and perhaps waiting up for her, they wouldn't do well to enter together. It was decided then, that Charissa

seek her way inside via the back, rather than *with* Em through the fore. And so it went, the vampiress waiting at a rear window for invitation to enter, and the witchling casting a simple opening spell to make access via the front door. Once inside, all was still and quiet – no one apparently about. Em slipped through the house to the back, opening up for Charissa. She stood fixed in place, wanting to cross the threshold, but unable.

"What are you waiting for?" Emily pressed in a whisper. "Come in here, please."

"Thank you, *that's* what I was waiting for. I can't enter unless invited," explained Charissa.

"Excuse me, what? I don't understand."

"I don't comprehend it either, my friend. I think of it as akin to Christ not coming into a soul to renew life unless *invited* to do so. Since I was *dead,* and am now of 'un-life,' I suspect something of the same rules apply, in some twisted, reverse order. That's the best I've been able to come up with anyway. Now, shall we find your basement? It *is* getting lighter in here with each passing moment – "

"Yes, of course, sorry. This way," Emily answered, lifting up the trap door to below, as they were already where the basement entry lay. "What will happen to you if you're in the light, Charissa? Do you waste away or something?"

"'Or something.' I've found that, depending upon exposure time, first I'll be nauseated, then a rash, then skin boils. I've never explored beyond that, and do not wish to, thank you."

"I wouldn't imagine," responded Emily, gesturing the way forward for her vampire friend to descend down below. As Charissa did, Em continued, asking, "Any sign of Andrea?"

"No, I'm not seeing or sensing her, but – " she stopped short, becoming aware of *another,* muffled presence within.

Kate – bound and gagged, there in the darkness.

Before either could properly react, Emily was pulled away, screaming, from her perch there atop the basement door; as it was quickly slammed shut, sealing Charissa and Kate inside together.

Robert

– clearly returned home – having baited and set the trap to secure both witches and the vampire, and still very much under the influence of Andrea. She came forth as well, starring coldly into Emily's eyes, asserting, "You'll be *silent,* witchling – now. You'll cast *no* spells to aid in either your escape or theirs' down there. You *will* do as a daughter should – and *obey* your father in whatever he tells you henceforth." Turning to Robert, she went on, "Mr. Laydon, sir, I require another room in your abode to myself for the day; preferably with no windows, if at all possible. Please rally your servants to see to my needs, thank you."

With that, Emily became as docile as a sheep, while the basement door was locked down tight, securing the two latest prisoners of Robert's 'dungeon.'

• • • •

Chapter 31

Erika

P rior to dawn's arrival, just a while after Emily and Charissa had left for the return to Clarksville, Erika had tried some more to talk with Jed. He had finally settled down from his earlier shock and confusion, and was trying to understand what his daughter attempted to say. Further and further she struggled with grunts and groans coming out instead of words. Finally, in frustration, she managed, *"Gt Iki!"*

"'Get Ishki'?" he asked back.

She shook her head with an affirmative howl. He went to retrieve Tanyee, while Erika remained there, knowing full well that this state of metamorphosis wouldn't do anything but cause fear and disturbance in the village. It wasn't her plan to return anyway; that's what she wanted her mother for. As a strong woman of the tribal spirits, Erika suspected *she* might have a good chance of understanding her *mentally*, as Emily did. She wanted to tell her of she and Nash's increasing instincts to depart altogether and go after Em and the vampire(s). They both felt like they 'smelled trouble brewing.'

Erika wanted to try this *before* returning to pure wolf form at first light, while the closer-to-human faculties were more to the fore. In a short while, she had her opportunity as Jed returned with Tanyee. Though Jed had told of some of the strange events of the night, nothing could prepare her for the state-of-being Erika was currently in. Tanyee audibly gasped upon seeing her, but settled herself down in short order, and approached her daughter, reaching out.

Erika reached back – gently – so as not to frighten her mother with any swift motions of her foreboding claws. Erika lightly touched Tanyee's head, in an effort to connect, and the mother instinctively did likewise. Erika closed her eyes and focused her thoughts.

"Ishiki, can you hear me? In your mind? I can't talk aloud – "

"I can hear you, oshetik," Tanyee answered out loud. "Speak to me..."

"Good. I'm rather stuck in this phase between wolf and human, and the vocal cords didn't quite make it to verbal function. Emily's spell-cast almost worked, but

something went wrong. Robert showed up with another vampire, which may have thrown things off."

"Wait, what? *Another* vampire? I wasn't aware there was a first one! Please, Erika, what's going on? And where *is* Emily anyway?"

*"She went off with the **first** one, who's her friend from Clarksville, and now they've gone back there, after Robert and the second one, the evil one."*

"So – her *friend,* the vampire, *is not* evil, and the other one *is?*" Tanyee repeated to get it straight, doubt pushing through her words as they came out, in the ridiculousness they sounded like when spoken aloud.

*"I don't understand **all** of it,"* Erika thought to her, the brainwave's tone terse, *"I've not exactly been my normal self, and have not been privy to everything going on with Em, I'm sorry. I'm just telling you what happened as I saw it. And now I'm telling you that I'm going after them, back to Clarksville myself. **Both** Nashoba and I feel it – they're going into danger, and will need our help."*

"You will not! You 'speak' to me of the witchery of your cousin, her 'friend' the vampire, and Robert, whose lunacy needs *no* introduction; and say you're going after them? I think not. I don't care how formidable you might be as you are, you're staying right here!"

Though he could only hear one side of the conversation, it was clear to Jed what was being said by Erika in thought to her mother, based on Tanyee's adamant responses. "I will go with her," he offered. "I have unfinished business with Robert regardless; he needs to be dealt with for his hand in all of this, and *I* need to be the one to do it. We'll be fine together. Besides, Erika returns to normal wolf form, as Nash, at dawn."

"And what of the 'vampires'?" Tanyee pressed.

"One is friend, one is foe," Jed offered to offset her worries, "so the deck is very well stacked to our favor; three-to-one on that count, and one-on-one with me and Robert."

"And you are good with those odds? You like your chances versus your brother?"

"I do. It's my job, and he must pay."

"Well – you two sound very determined and committed to this. Who am I to argue, besides wife and mother? Go then, save your friends, seek your vengeance, and be done with it! Just be sure my oshetik returns in one piece!"

"Maybe we'll even return with her fully restored," Jed added. "Emily wasn't giving up on the incomplete spell."

"I should hope not. Certainly I am grateful for her hand in bringing Erika back, though in strange fashion, even for *our* beliefs. But still, to be stuck like this *in between* wolf and girl – isn't right."

Erika took no offense to her mother's words – she felt the same way. She was dealing with it, but it wasn't easy. Although, being able to stand up to a vampire wasn't bad! And to that point, hers and Nash's instincts that they'd be needed for such, would almost certainly come into play. Thus, after a heartfelt good-bye with Tanyee, the two started their trek from the Chickasaw lands towards the settlement of Clarksville. By the time they were closing in towards the town, the moon had gone down and the sun had come up, bringing with it Erika's reversion back to normal wolf form as Nashoba.

• • • •

Now, in this day and time, within this pre-state, the practice of sorcery or witchcraft was dealt with a little more legally than it was one hundred years ago, in Salem for example. An official accusation would be made to an authority; it would be investigated and finally brought to trial if it held up. Tennessee was something of a hotbed of activity in this respect; the Taylors of the Fentress County Witchcraft Trial, and the infamous Bell Witch. As such, when Robert Laydon openly sought to call out his daughter for practicing, it was not by means of a public display in the town's square for hanging; no, the constable came to their house to visit and listen to the formal charge being brought against her.

About the time Jed and 'NashErka' were arriving to the outskirts of the Laydons' premises, they spied Robert leading a lawman inside. This was curious they thought; giving ever more credence to the bad vibes Erika and Nash already had, prompting them to come. 'Nash' nudged Jed to move in closer. They both did, nestling up towards a window to get a look at what was going on inside. It wasn't good. Emily was seated to the side of her father, while he was next to the constable. She looked hopeless, sad, and more docile than Erika had ever seen her before. Robert looked to be on a rant, arms gesturing about wildly, occasionally pointing at Em, with a grimace.

Erika thought, given their proximity, she might try reaching out with Nash's mind once more to try and communicate with Em mentally. Jed noticed the wolf going quiet and focused, and presumed that's what they were up to, having seen it done before with Tanyee. Therefore, he went on even closer alert to what was going on both inside and out, should anyone else venture outside and spot them. Robert *did* have a full enough household with both family and slaves.

"Emily, do you hear me?" Erika thought to her. *"Father and I are here. With the other vampire having escaped, I sensed trouble on the horizon, so we came. What's going on in there?"*

"I hear you," Emily thought back. *"You shouldn't have come, but I'm glad you did. Charissa and I came to the house; it seemed empty, so I showed her to the basement for the daytime. As we did, father grabbed **me**, then sealed Chris away with mother, who he'd already put down there. I think he's still under Andrea's control."*

"Wonderful. So he's got all three of you. Why does he have you in the room with him and a lawman?"

"Because he's charging me and mother with practicing witchcraft. It's how it's done these days. He's even claiming that a spell of mine caused 'the accident' with you, can you believe it?"

"Why then, are you just sitting there, Em?"

"Because Andrea has compelled me to obey him and be cooperative. Plus, he already has Mother and Charissa prisoner downstairs. From what he's saying, I fear he's going to bring Chris up into the light to show him what kind of 'demon' she is."

*"So, you are saying that, just as **I** only become a wolf-woman under the moon, Charissa cannot be in the light of day?"*

"Yes, that's right, it's a part of her 'curse.'"

*"If **that's** true, then maybe we can force this 'Andrea' out into the light as well..."*

But, it was not to be, at least not now certainly. For, at that moment, amidst the cerebral conversation of the cousins, Charissa appeared in the hallway, adjoining the room wherein Robert, the lawman, and Emily sat. She seemed hesitant in her forward progress to come into their presence, but move she did, wincing to the room's increasing light.

Chapter 32

Charissa

Some minutes before I found myself entering the Laydon's front room, I'd been unexpectedly awoken in the basement space I now shared with Kate. At first, I'd been awake for a while; this turn of events not the sort of thing that makes for immediate rest. But eventually I did slumber, so when Andrea entered later, stirring both of us awake, I for one, wasn't ready for it. Furthermore, my progeny's stealthy appearance made for a smart way to get what she wanted, taking me unawares. Otherwise, I'd have pounced on her immediately, and she knew it.

As it was, she moved directly and quickly upon Kate, holding her by the throat with threats that she'd kill her if I didn't cooperate. What she wanted me to do, I'd no idea, but I soon found out. As I ascended from out of our 'dungeon' and out towards where Emily, Robert and a constable were gathered, it became clear I was being presented as an accomplice to Em's witchery.

Upon entry, I came into a conversation that was presumably a formal charge of witchcraft against Emily. And, as further evidence, I was being pushed into light exposure so that my deterioration would be observed, and more than likely concluded to be signs of my own 'dark tendencies,' paired along with those of Emily's. Between both Robert and Andrea, I had to credit them a well-orchestrated scheme for our demise. Now I just needed a way to make sure that didn't become a reality.

"Now just watch, Jones," Robert began, speaking to the lawman. "Watch and see what happens to the kind of creature my daughter has taken to summoning with the dark magic. The woman looks beautiful, doesn't she? But she won't in a few minutes..."

No, I wouldn't. He'd certainly made certain his little gathering was in the brightest room of the house, sunlight pouring in from everywhere. I was already feeling sick, and soon the rashes would start. I just prayed they wouldn't actually take me outside. But again, congrats to him on piling it on with imagination: '...creature my daughter has taken to summoning,' oh, please. If I wasn't getting sick already, *that* alone would've made me! Besides the light, what was really starting to make me ill were the poor choices Andrea had accused me of making consistently. It would stand to reason that, somehow, I should have been able to make better ones along the way to keep myself out of predicaments such as this.

But here I was, standing before them, my skin blotching, and bumps starting to form. Between the queasiness and all of that, I had to lean down to my knees and support myself upon the arm of where Emily was seated. She may have been being compelled, but our closeness in the moment certainly got her speaking up –

"Stop it!" shouted Em, taking my hand there next to her. "Can't you see the light is hurting her? Let her alone and take her back downstairs,

please!"

"Oh, you'd like that wouldn't you, Emily?" Robert returned, glaring at her. "This foul woman duped me from the moment I met her, feigning concern for me just to get to you so you could conspire together and lead me to see, God knows *what,* out there in my damn brother's adopted land!"

"You're not that hard to 'dupe', Robert," I said with fading energy. "You're being duped by my progeny even now, you fool; doing this to me, even your own family. This is extreme, sir, even for you!"

"'Progeny'?" he asked, confused. "What the devil are you talking about?"

"She 'made' Andrea, Father!" Emily snapped. "And now, *she's* turned on Charissa, compelling you to do her bidding to divide us all!"

"*You* made the choice that would divide 'us all' when you started practicing sorcery, daughter." Robert then turned back to Constable Jones to see how he was being swayed by all of our unfathomable chatter. "Well, Jones? You see? Their dark dealings are so deep I, for one, can't make heads or tails of what they are going on about. What do you think?"

"Robert," he began, "I don't know *what* you've gotten yourself in the middle of here, but it definitely ain't right. I say we bring 'em in and throw both of 'em in a cell for now, and then proceed from there. And what about the wife, Bob? You'd said she was one of 'em too?"

"I'll deal with her myself for now," was Robert's only reply.

Perfect, and well played. Keep one of us left behind for leverage to make sure the rest stay in line. And his wife to boot; the lawman wouldn't question that. For an idiot, Robert was adequately cunning.

So much so that if the lawman wasn't quite convinced yet, he surely would be when they dragged me to the jail in the direct sunlight, and this would all plummet to ghastly depths *I* wasn't even aware of yet. God help me. At least Emily would be by my side, but that's the best of the situation I could come up with.

· · · ·

Emily was literally *at* my side, shouldering me to my right while Jones supported me on the left as we hobbled through the settlement to the jailhouse. Robert wouldn't deign to touch me. Couldn't say as I blamed him, the mess I was coming to be. The skin boils were fully present now, some of them even popping and bleeding. I could see that some of my hair was beginning to fall out as well, plus I'd periodically begun to gag, with associated vomiting spells spewing up, of course, blood.

I began to imagine what it might have been like for Christ, attempting to carry the heavy load of one of the cross beams after having been beaten and flogged. The trip to Golgotha must have seemed endless to him, just as this much shorter trip across town seemed to me. Now I longed for that jail cell!

"You see, Jones?" Robert began, as we thankfully neared our destination. "So dark is she that she withers away when facing the light of day, of God! Only He knows for sure what kind of witch-demon she might be. At least my daughter can still withstand the sun!"

"Don't know how you discovered this, Bob," Jones replied, "but you've done the whole town a favor considering she's been serving us at the pub for a while now. We'd have never known!"

So, Jones remembered me! He should've, inasmuch as he'd been one of the men I'd taken to my room once, convincing him he'd 'had a good time' with me. But he certainly wasn't admitting to that.

"Go shag yourself, Robert," I spat to his comments. Turning to my side, I looked at Jones and continued, "You too, wanker."

With that, upon our arrival to the gaol, he heaved me hard into the cell, while Robert held Emily back from me to avoid the same mistreatment to his daughter. She pulled away from him violently and ran in to attend to me.

"Birds of a feather," Jones said as he closed the door on us, then proceeded to walk away with Robert, leaving us to ourselves.

Emily approached me gingerly, hesitant to touch just about anywhere as it was all peeling, oozing, and bloody flesh. It wasn't pretty, and I'm normally told that I *am*.

"How can I help you, Charissa? I don't know what to do, where to start. You said this would be bad, but I didn't realize – "

"How bad it really was?" I completed for her. "This *is* about the worst ever. I've never actually been forced into the light for so long of an exposure. I guess now we both know *how* bad. What can you do, you ask? Well, I'd start with whatever little spells of healing you might have up your sleeve; and then – "

"Yes?"

"You'd be a darling and a savior if you'd allow me to – drink of you."

She looked a little taken aback, but not surprised really. When you associate yourself with a vampire, and they're in a bad way, it's progressive math to assume blood will be needed eventually. There was that look of concern in her eyes though, which I quickly addressed, "Worry *not* Emily, I won't be 'turning' you; I'll only have enough for sustenance, to get my strength back. Turning someone is a more involved process, the *co-mingling* of one another's blood, not just the mere taking of it, you see."

"'I see,' I suppose," she said. "All right, let's just get to that first, and I'll work on a healing spell after. That okay with you?"

"Perfect."

At first, as is natural for people, she bore her neck out to me. I waved her off as I did not want bite marks visible for when Robert would undoubtedly see her later. I declined her wrist as well for the same reason, settling upon the veins of her ankle. Strange, probably, that I'd be concerned with cosmetics when in such a sorry state as I was. But I'd already brought Emily enough grief, and I didn't want to add to it when it was perfectly avoidable. And so it was that I drank deeply of the young witch. She was very good, and the magically-infused blood was more potent than I could have imagined. So much so that when she was chanting a healing mantra as I drank, it transposed beautifully through the blood itself, helping me improve almost immediately!

Though it was all about rejuvenating me from exposure in this meal, I observed a stark difference in the process, having feasted upon someone I was close to. No matter how you look at it, drinking lifeblood from another *is* intimate. And the fact that I cared for Emily made this *more* than mere food. It was like taking in and feeling her *essence;* and the fact that she too was a supernatural only enhanced it. And I believe she was feeling it also when I finished, as we both

flushed in the aftermath.

"My goodness, I feel much better, Em," I said. "You are *very* tasty!"

"You look a lot better too, Chris," she replied, brushing some strands of returned-luster hair out of my face. "And though a jail cell isn't ideal, by its very nature, it's almost as good as the basement for being more away from the light. So, if they leave us alone till dark, I can do a simple 'unlock spell' and we can be out of here. I can even throw up a cloaking spell, and no one will be the wiser in our movements beyond here."

"Excellent, witchling. That will be most helpful when we return to rescue your mother; and I'm sure Andrea will expect just such a move.

"Yes, well, what she *won't* be expecting is Jed and Erika. They're here, Charissa! I didn't get a chance to tell you earlier, but just before you were called up from the basement, *she* was talking to me inside my mind, just as you and I have through dreams. We've done *that,* she and I, since we were kids; so now it's easy since she's crossed over, then back again, as Nashoba. Come nightfall and the second night of the full moon, she should morph back into the wolf-girl creature again, giving us an unanticipated advantage!"

"*Most* excellent, Emily! I will tell you this: Should circumstances unfold to where Erika, in wolf-beast form, should grapple with Andrea again, I won't stop her this time. My progeny's behavior in all of this has earned her whatever death she has coming, no matter by *who's* hand!"

Emily looked at me in all seriousness to this pronouncement; now realizing by my harsh words that the gloves were off. I no longer cared who had blood on their hands. I'd now been pushed back to my more animalistic instincts and was more than ready to see Andrea's end, regardless of whether I, or another, accomplished it. It just needed to get done. Period.

Speaking of Andrea – *and* Emily – I noticed that the commands I'd overheard Andrea give Em at the time we both fell into her trap, seemed to have worn off. Em was clearly moving beyond the bounds of obeying Robert now. Perhaps being in *my* presence, Andrea's *maker,* trumped whatever directives she'd previously given to her. On that note, a thought occurred, more of a suggestion rather than something I'd *compel* her to do.

"Emily, since we have at least half the day left before sundown, might it not behoove you to cast and remove yourself from here now, apart from me? If Jed and Erika *are* here, would it not be more strategic for you to locate and coordinate with them presently; not waste the day away staying here with me?"

"I don't want to leave you, but you're probably right," she agreed. "You and I *know* what our plan is – but they don't. All of us being on the same page is what's going to make the difference in besting Andrea and my father."

I nodded in agreement and hugged her.

· · · ·

Chapter 33

Erika

Having reluctantly concurred with Charissa, Emily strode out of and away from the jailhouse, through town, toward her destination of home. She couldn't be sure that's where she'd still find her cousin and uncle, but that *was* the last place she'd known that they'd been. It seemed to her the most natural place to start. She made her way unfettered and unseen as her 'cloak' was once again working perfectly.

As she approached the outskirts of their land, she could see Nashoba's silhouette sitting stoically in the distance, looking, it appeared, towards the woods beyond. Curious. A comforting thought then crossed Em's mind. Having just left Charissa's company, she thought of *her* – seeing herself and Nashoba for the first time, as the vampire had described of her first sighting of them. Observing from a goodly distance such as her own field of view right now. Somehow, this recollection seemed appropriately ironic to her in *this* moment, as the cousins were about to join together once again.

*"Cousin, shouldn't you be looking more the **other** direction, towards the house?"* Em began thinking to Nasherka as she neared them. *"If there's any trouble, it's going to come from there..."*

"'Trouble' has already begun into the woods, cousin," Erika thought back, turning about to greet Emily's embrace as she dropped her cloak and stooped to hug Nash. *"My Inki has gone after **your** father. We watched earlier as you and poor Charissa were taken into town somewhere. Later, Robert returned alone, went inside, came back out with a rifle, and proceeded into the forest. I suspect he went to blow off steam hunting, but Inki decided to go after him, without me. He wanted to deal with his brother all by himself."*

"Our fathers set out against each other. How Cain and Abel," thought Emily. *"Well, I'll say this at least – it simplifies things for us in terms of our focus here. Unfortunately, it's not quite dusk yet, so no 'wolf-woman' version of you yet, nor Charissa's availability."*

*"How **is** she, Em? Last I saw of her wasn't good."*

"*She is improved. Being in the dungeon-like atmosphere of a jail cell's lessened light helped, my healing chants aided, but giving her my blood to drink did the most good of all.*"

"*You did that? You are a good friend.*"

"**She** *is too – she shared a wonderful idea for returning* **you** *to full human form during the moon phase. Perhaps after all of this is taken care of, by tomorrow night's third full moon, we can try it and maybe return you completely to yourself! I'll tell you all about it later.*"

"*Very well, that's encouraging! What's your plan in the meantime? I'd still like to go after Inki...*"

"*You should – while I go back to the house, cloaked, to check on Mother, perhaps try to get her out of there...*"

"*Alone? No, I'll go with you, in case you encounter Andrea again. You'll need every advantage you can, and Inki can handle Robert.*"

. . . .

There was more bustle inside the Laydon home by this time, as the day had worn on. Isaiah and Ben went to and fro from inside to out in their tasks, while Clare was all about her maid duties within. *All* of them though, remained perplexed at the odd goings-on of the day. From the strange woman's appearance, to Robert's entertaining of the constable and accusations upon Emily, to the strangest of all – Kate's continued absence around the house over the course of the day. It appeared she'd been shut away, and Robert was answerable to no one when it came to his household. If he'd deigned to put up his wife or toss his daughter in jail, it was his prerogative and therefore unquestionable.

Stranger still was Robert's return after taking Emily and her friend away; then leaving once more with his rifle out into the woods. The other unknown female who'd they'd prepared a room for had now vacated it, and went they knew not where. This was the atmosphere Emily encountered when she'd re-entered the house, invisible to all. Would she remain that way if she *did* encounter Andrea again? Or would the progeny vampire see through her cloak, being a paranormal herself? She hoped she wouldn't have to find out as she apprehensively re-opened the basement door once more. As it turned out, she *wouldn't* gain answer to that question as the basement was – empty.

Where had they gone, Mother and Andrea? There was *no* better place for the vampiress to be than inside during the daytime. *How* could she

be gone? And why was Kate missing too? Something had to have occurred since she'd been away and Robert had left. It was time to 'de-cloak' and go get the answer from the one who'd most likely know – Clare.

Materializing from invisibility to perceivable was like a ghost appearing out of thin air. Emily did so as she spoke Clare's name, coming into the servant woman's sight, scaring the bejesus out of her.

"Holy Jesus!" Clare shrieked, nearly jumping out of her skin. *"That* ain't natural, girl. And I knows you didn't walk into the room just now – that was some 'spell trickery' of yours that yer pappy rightly accused you of! Don't be scarin' me like that. What'chu want?"

"What I *want* is for you to tell me where Mother and that woman went to. I know you watch things like a hawk around here; because I've a pretty good notion you've spied on me and mother, helping my father track me when I'd leave to go see my cousin."

"Don't know what you talkin' 'bout, girl. I don't see nuthin', I don't says nuthin.'"

"Liar," Emily spat, moving up close into Clare's personal space. "I know you think I'm an ignorant, privileged little white girl, but I'm not as blind as you believe. Now, out with it, where did they go?"

"I dunno," Clare persisted.

As quickly as she'd just gotten in the woman's face, Em whirled about and dashed to the back door, opening it and snapping her fingers. "Nashoba, come!" she barked. A second later, the wolf appeared, stepping inside with a foreboding growl. "This way, boy," Em directed, having Nash fall in stride with her, returning to Clare. She gasped in terror as they approached her.

"Now Clare, I don't believe you've met my wolf yet, have you? This is Nashoba, who also happens to be the host for my cousin Erika's spirit. For the last time, tell me what I want before they make you into one of the meals you cook in this kitchen!"

"All right, Em, damn! I'll tell you already! That lady had come outta the basement a while ago, lookin' for yer pappy. I tol' her she jus' missed him, that he'd gone stalkin' off with his gun into the woods. So, she goes back down, then comes back up 'wit yer mum after a bit. As they's goes to the door, they start fadin' out from sight, just like you did when you came outta nowhere just now! Now, I knows yer mum used ta mess with the craft long time ago, but it sure looked to me like she's back doin' it again! It's been one God-forsaken day 'round here, and all o' that just confounded me even more. Any o' that mean anything to you, girl?"

Emily paused, trying to digest it all. Nasherka looked up at her as if looking for that same answer themselves. It took a moment to process, but slowly Emily began to form a theory.

"Clare, you said they *both* were fading from sight as the left, right?"

"Uh huh."

"I think – Andrea wanted Mom to use a cloaking spell, not just to be invisible from sight, but *also* to cloak *her **from*** the sun! If she was looking for Father but couldn't find him, she might've felt like her control over him might slip after a time away from each other. Maybe she's going to look for him *now,* back out in the woods."

"Or," Erika thought to Em, *"perhaps she's going into town after Charissa; **not** waiting for nightfall to deal with her – or **me.**"*

"Good point, cousin," Em answered aloud, not thinking. "Let's return to our original plan then. You go back into the woods, see if they've gone in our fathers' direction, and I'll go back into town and see if they are going after Chris."

"Who you talkin' to, Em?" asked Clare. "Don't tell me you's talkin' to the ghost *in* the wolf!"

Emily just looked at her and grinned.

· · · ·

Nasherka loped through the surrounding forest, taking proper care to be stealthy, yet speedy all at once. They didn't need to be charging in so fast as to alert those they sought to their incoming presence; but neither did they have time to waste. They. It was both odd and exhilarating simultaneously to be in this unison state-of-being, wolf and girl as one. Human soul and intelligence remained, integrated with all the animal's instincts and senses. And *both* personalities retained. It was a strange and wondrous thing altogether. Effective too, for, before long, they'd located the brothers; but that was all. No vampiress and no mother witch.

Jed and Robert, however were themselves found to be in the middle of a raging fight; one that was beginning to wane towards Jed's advantage – as she'd predicted. Just as when she'd intervened in the battle between Andrea and Charissa, Erika observed her father pinning Robert to the ground in like fashion. She was suddenly filled with a daughter's pride in her 'inki' that made her feel like a cheerleader while she watched. Her acute wolf hearing was able to discern their conversation even from the distance between them.

"We've left each other alone for many years, Robert, despite the

festering wound created by your incessant prejudice. I've let it go all this time; but what you've done now, and what you're continuing to do, has pushed me to *have* to contend with you. This can no longer go unanswered! You killed my daughter, for Christ's sake! Then had the audacity to blame it on one of Emily's spells!"

Robert looked at him aghast, confounded by *how* he could possibly know that.

"Yes, brother, I *know* because I have 'inside news' that reaches me from beyond Erika's grave! *She* spoke of this to me from her conversations with Emily. Em, who, if *not* for her magic, would see me as a truly bereaved father. As it is, I *still* have connection with her, because *she* has union in and through her wolf, who *Em* bonded her spirit to. I know you believe it all to be of the Devil, but you know what I believe? *You're* the devil! Conspiring with a wicked vampire and trying to further banish your daughter for practicing the magic that has allowed Erika to remain on this plane with us!" That said, Jed hammered a couple more punches into his brother's face. Jed paused as more blood poured from Robert's nose and mouth. "Why did you come out here by yourself," he continued, "after throwing Em and Charissa in jail anyway?"

"Because I needed to get away from all this mess for a while and just shoot at something," admitted Robert. "You're right, it's gotten out-of-hand, and it's too much. I've put Em in jail and Kate in the basement, and that woman, whatever she is, controlling what goes on in *my* house. Don't get me wrong, my wife and daughter cannot be allowed to practice witchcraft under my roof, but the disarray Andrea is causing has gone too far."

"Finally, some sense out of you," replied Jed. "But don't think for a minute that uttering one slight compromise from your iron will is going to change how I'm going to deal with you. You are coming with me!" He hefted Robert up and began tying his hands behind his back along with a tethering piece of rope to guide him along as they prepared to head back.

Seeing all of this, Erika felt secure that her inki had the situation well in hand, and whatever he was going to with Robert would be a sound decision. So, with that, she turned and loped back off to return back towards Clarksville to reunite with Emily to help her in any way she could.

Chapter 34
Charissa

I have to confess, the next visitor I had in my cozy little cell was not who I expected it to be. I might well have anticipated Robert or Jones, a deputy perhaps, maybe Emily's return, or even Erika's arrival. It wasn't that the visitors who *did* show up weren't on my list at all, it's just that I could have never conceived *Andrea* coming here while the sun was still up. The fact that she was here with Kate in tow was making me think there might be some connection there, but I couldn't quite put my finger on it.

"Ooohh, confused are you, my maker?" said Andrea sarcastically, immediately addressing her apparent victory over the daylight. "Wondering, I'll wager, how I'm able to be out in the daytime? It *is* kind of nice, actually. These witches have the ability to do the 'cloaking spell,' you know. That got me thinking that if they can shield themselves from visibility, perhaps they so too could shield such as us against the light. Initially, my 'friend' Kate here blended the two spells so that when we left the Laydons' house vanishing into thin air, the shield simultaneously went up, making me 'invisible' to the sun itself! Isn't that just marvelous?"

"I'm very happy for you," I replied with equal sarcasm. "What are you doing here, Andrea?"

"Well, as you know, Robert has been my key pawn in this whole endeavor so far, but inasmuch as I've been unable to locate the fool, and I've little patience nor time, I've since moved on. The lawman will serve just as well. I'm having dear Kate here refine 'the sun-shield' so to speak, to where I'll retain visibility while still maintaining the protection – *so that* I can be center-stage *with* Jones whilst we do a little 'public trial' for you 'witches.' Oh yes, we'll show to the townsfolk just what happens to 'evil' creatures such as yourself – when I throw you back out into the sun again, *without a shield,* in front of everyone! Then we'll have ourselves a little lynching. Perhaps even a burning at the stake – for *you.* I'm thinking that's the only thing which will put one of *us* down, don't you think, Charissa?"

I said nothing, I had no words. I was simply too astonished at the lengths her madness had now reached in what she was planning. And it all came back to me – I'm the one who *made* her. It amused me at the time; my own little sense of 'playful' vengeance, shall we say. Now it seemed, I would be paying the ultimate price for my little 'distraction.' Worse still, *others* were paying the penalty right along with me. Better I should have stayed in my homeland and faced the consequences to my crimes; not bring me *and* my mistake across the ocean to torment these poor people – my friends.

"Well, don't just sit there commiserating over it all, Charissa!" Andrea interrupted into my thoughts. "Hop to it and get up now! I want to get moving!"

"Why should I, Andrea? Because you'll threaten to kill Kate? You plan to kill us both anyway, so what's the difference?"

"The *difference is,*" she began in answer, putting a hand to Kate's throat, "that in cooperating, you're *delaying* your deaths. And within that delay, who knows? Emily or Robert could return and attempt your rescues. Away from me this long, his submission to me may well have worn off and he'll seek to save his wife, even if she is a witch. But, dear Charissa – resist me now and I'll snap Kate's neck right here; and where she might have had a chance if you'd followed directions, she'll have *none* because you didn't do as you were told! I don't think little Emily's endearment to you will go much further upon learning her mother's life could've been prolonged if not for your stubbornness."

"Very well," I reluctantly agreed. She was logical even in her madness.

"As a bonus, Charissa, I'll have Kate do the 'sun shield' for you as well, as we venture onward to 'the trial.'"

"And why would you do that for me? Why do any of this, Andrea?"

"*Because,* my dear maker, I only seek to emulate *you.* Your massacre of the priests in London was sheer genius! All of this is merely my attempt to achieve equal brilliance."

"Excuse me, ladies, if I may – " Kate began. "The 'sun shield' spell, as you call it, is difficult to cast and maintain, even over one person, let alone two. I haven't practiced in years, and doing *that* much was already a chore. I'm not sure I can – "

"Do your best, witch," Andrea replied. "If you fail, fail on *her.* If she starts to degrade in the light before our arrival, so be it. Just maintain *me* then. I command it." She added that at the end simply to reassert the compulsion over Kate, I think, just in case it had been in any way

waning. She wasn't taking any chances.

And she was right. I *did* have the opportunity here to belay our deaths, and Emily was out there somewhere. The plan was to seek out her cousin once more; and in all likelihood, she'd probably returned to the house toward that end. If so, she'd know by now that we were gone, and would probably be formulating some kind of effort to find us again. And though this was all entirely conjecture on my part, I felt it *did* have substance. So, what choice did I have really? I *had* to acquiesce to my mad progeny's insanity, at least for now.

As we exited the gaol, we came again upon lawman Jones, who was apparently returning to confer with Andrea, as townsfolk moved past us as well. "As ya can see," he said, "I've got people on the move towards the end of town for this meetin' or whatever, out by the oaks. I see ya got our 'favorite' barmaid still here, but where's Emily? Oh, and hi Mrs. Laydon, sorry 'bout all this," he said to Kate in closing.

"No sorrier than I am, Carl," she replied, calling him by first name. Turning to both of us vampires, she continued, "Well, ladies? Do *either* of you have an answer to his question, because I certainly have *no* idea where my daughter is at this point," she said sternly, "and I would dearly like to know!"

For the first time in a long time, Andrea and I were both in unison, we didn't know. We looked at each other with unknown and accusing glances as if each blaming the other for the girl's absence. Finally, I replied with the only true, honest answer. "She left earlier via an unlocking and cloaking spell. I suspect she went back to your home, Kate, to check on you, rescue you perhaps, from the clutches of my

'child' here." Clearly, there had been more to it than that, but I wasn't about to give away any more information to the effect of our additional allies. "Obviously she missed you as you are now both here with me." That said, Andrea glared at me all the more, as though sensing it was wasn't the whole truth.

Then she added, "And perhaps, finding no one there, she went on to look for the old man herself, just as I did; but in not finding him, we came here instead." Finally, in effort to continue to wear Kate down, she added, "She's probably going to exact due vengeance upon that fool for all he's done to disrupt your family." Kate turned from Andrea in disgust, wishing to brook no more of her little jabs, as did I.

"He's her father," Kate mumbled more to me than to Andrea, though her words were in answer to what my progeny had said, "she may be angry with him, but I doubt she'll kill him."

"Don't be so sure, Kate," I replied. "A while back, I think she was hoping *I* would do it for her. I wouldn't have minded actually, but I preferred to see he and Emily restored at some point." As we'd closed a little distance between ourselves and Andrea, walking confidently ahead of her, I continued, whispering so quietly even another vampire couldn't hear. "But don't worry, that's *not* what she's up to. She's seeking out Erika and Jed, not Robert. They're here to help. And besides, as far as *our* little predicament here, don't fret to that, either. I have a plan."

Kate brightened somewhat to all of this as we continued building a gap between Andrea and us. It didn't last long.

"Just *where* do you two think you're going? Don't presume to walk away from me!" She was suddenly to our rear again and upon us like

lightening, with a blow to the back of my head and a hand round Kate's throat. "You asked before *why* I'm doing this, Charissa. You just showed me a good example of why, walking away from me like that, with your '*new* friend.' That's what *we* were once, if you remember – friends. Good ones. And it all fell apart over a stupid man. Don't think for a minute I'm unique in how far I'm going with all this. Your vengeance upon me and James, not to mention the priests, was just as warped."

"Yes," I returned, "but there comes a time when you cease and desist from it all and move on, Andrea."

"Of course," she replied, "*after* it is complete, just as you did. Mine will be shortly as you'll see, and then I'll 'move on,' as you say. Unfortunately for you two, *you won't.*"

Chapter 35
Em-Erika

Against all sage advice, Isaiah, from the Laydons' house, insisted upon going to join Emily as she plodded back into town. Despite even her own objections, the slave boy would not take no for an answer. So, by the time she reached the jail again, she had company, which ultimately, she *was* thankful for. At this point, the day had finally begun to wane on towards dusk, which meant who she was here to see would finally be able 'to come out and play.'

If she were there.

And she wasn't.

Charissa was gone, and Emily's mind went into a tizzy. Where could she be – and where in tarnation was everybody else; her mother, the townsfolk – *everyone!* She'd waltzed back into the jailhouse unencumbered, no one there to even ask what her business was, or why a slave boy was out with her in public. And all around the rest of the settlement, there was no one to be seen. It was as if everybody there had gone to gather for some 'township event' or something. Waitaminute. Oh no. That might be it exactly.

An old-fashioned, public – 'witch trial.'

But it wasn't *done* that way anymore though, Emily mused. Then again, it wasn't every day you had vampires around who could compel people to do things. With both her mother and her friend gone, it was a good bet that was just what Andrea might be up to, especially if she'd found a magical solution to the daylight problem via Mother. Something Em herself was going to need to provide for Charissa if any of this conjecture were true. And it was time to find out. She cast a locator spell which revealed a large gathering at the end of town along the line of large Bur Oak trees. Perfect for a hanging if that's indeed what they were up to.

But *not* if she had anything to say about it.

Before long, Emily and Isaiah had skulked their way in that direction and to said destination. They hunkered in behind some other trees and bushes, observing exactly the scene she'd imagined and feared. Andrea next to lawman

Jones, spouting off theories and accusations while pointing at the two behind them, a bound Kate and Charissa, easily swaying the crowd before them. Charissa was once again in a bad way, having dropped to her knees at this point, skin rashing and boiling, looking as though she were on the verge of total collapse.

To this, Em began to quietly chant and gesture toward Charissa. She had to be careful as she wasn't going for the typical cloaking spell, but rather more of a 'shield protection' spell from the sun, which was lowering, but not yet set, in the sky. Em noted, as she continued, that the moon too, was now becoming visible as well. Excellent. Perhaps they'd get the werewolf out of Erika a little early – and in this case, timely!

As she continued casting with one hand, she turned to Isaiah, taking his wrist with the other. "Isaiah, I need a favor. Go back through town and scout for me. Jed and his wolf will probably be on their way to us. They need to know what's going on *before* they get here. And Isaiah, there's something else. The wolf, when you see it, may be – something *more.* Something in between wolf and human. She may be changing by now, I'm not sure."

"She? Changing? What you talkin' 'bout, Em?"

"I'll explain later – for now, just go. And don't be afraid, the 'creature's' on our side!"

It was a good thing Emily had forewarned him about the 'changeling' state of the wolf. For, on the far end of town opposite them, Isaiah saw it for the first time. And Jed *was **not*** there with it. At least not yet. He watched, amazed and a little scared, as with each step, the wolf was beginning to morph. At first, its fur lessened just a tiny bit. Then, the limbs lengthened; particularly the front legs, becoming more like arms.

At that point, its slow trot towards him ceased. It hunkered down, moving to a dropped position, while those arms continued to fully form, paws becoming hands with claws. As the hind legs extended, the 'wolf' rose up to where it stood upon two bi-pedal feet. The face retracted to where the canine snout receded and the jawline blended into more of a below-the-cheeks facade. The face became more girlish as features softened and dark tresses began to fall from the scalp.

He wasn't sure how, but he had the strongest feeling that somehow, Em had something to do with this, what with all the witchcraft accusations being thrown at her. Suddenly, all the incomplete rumors he'd been hearing around the house about the 'death' of an Indian girl started kicking into his mind. Could this changeling beast in some way – be her?

The warning to this was one thing – *seeing* it, and it being before you was quite another. Isaiah tried to sturdy himself through his sudden fear, raising his arms in truce, then waving one arm to come follow him as he turned back around to return to Emily. The she-beast followed slowly as if sensing his fright, not moving too quickly so as not to scare him all the more. When she'd closed the gap to a few arms-length between them, she again tried to speak verbally and said, "Negro – boy. Wait – a – moment. Please."

That did it. The words, though coming out strained, were helping dispel his alarm. Tonight's change clearly had improved enough from last night to allow for understandable verbalization. "I'm – Erika, an Indian – girl. You – are owned by – Robert, my murderer – are you not?"

And there it was for Isaiah, the confirmation to that which he'd heard. It was all true then. "Yeah, Mr. Laydon's our 'massa. And yo killer I guesses. I's sorry, miss. But, how you go from bein' dead – to 'dis? Em be doin' the craft on you?"

"Yes," she replied, chuckling, which felt and sounded strange, emoting in this form. "Emily – bonded me to – my wolf – long before – I died. Then, I *did* – and my spirit – went to the wolf. I can tell you – more later – all right?"

"Yeah, 'dat's what Em said too," he replied, laughing also. In seeing how hard it was for her to speak fluidly, he agreed and concluded, "better later fo 'da rest anyways; there's some shi' goin' down outside o' town we gots ta 'git to right now."

Erika nodded, and they both continued on together, the black boy and Chickasaw wolf-girl, an interesting and ironic pair.

Chapter 36

Charissa

The sun was nearly down as Andrea had Jones start tying me to a tree trunk and his deputy prepare a noose around Kate's neck, which he then began looping across a branch of the same tree. She was intending for quite the show here. All the while this had been going on, I'd been improving from my time in the bright sun. As promised, Andrea had granted me a small respite from its rays, coaxing Kate to give me the 'shield' protection as we'd made our way here. But, for 'show,' she'd had her drop it once we'd arrived, so the people could see what happened to evil creatures such as we, in 'God's sunlight.' So easy to play upon the Puritan mindset. Therefore, as she'd rambled on, I'd begun to degrade yet again.

Here, however, is where it got interesting, and began to play into my tenuous 'plan.' As I began to get better once more, Andrea had likely assumed it was because the sun was going down. It may have been a factor, but I also sensed another protection spell-cast had come into effect. I'd already experienced what it felt like from when Kate did it, and I knew she couldn't be doing it now, because she'd been ordered to stop. So, it had to be – another witch. Which meant Emily was nearby, unseen. And with any luck, Erika might be here as well. And the moon *had* already come up, full and bright.

Andrea moved to make a final statement to her assemblage of sheep which she was controlling like a conductor of an orchestra. "The founding forefathers who'd come from England, just as I have, *knew* to brook no tolerance for those such as these in our midst; they who'd bring the darkness of demonology and witchcraft to our doors. Let not the slow justice of today – charges brought, jury of peers, and innocent till proven guilty – prevail. May we rather, as in the days of Salem a century ago, be swift and quick to put down all those who would dare to dabble against the good people of God's true light!"

Bloody hell, she knew how to lay it on thick; Robert would've loved it, were he here. The more she went on, the more I was determined to put *her* down, the little bitch. Still, I needed the right opening in order to take over this mob mentality she'd rallied and was playing like a fiddle. Unfortunately, it hadn't presented itself just yet, and we were running out of time. Once more, I prayed for the Holy Ghost who'd never arrived upon the isle of my turning – to come forth.

Then, as Jones lit the pyre round my feet, I saw, or sensed it – *in* the flames. *"And there appeared unto them cloven tongues like as of fire, and it sat upon each of them,"* – from Acts, if memory served.

'Each of them,' **Emily** *and* **Erika** emerged simultaneously;

Em bolting for Kate, spell casting against the now-taut noose round her mother's neck; and –

Erika launching herself again into Andrea, having seemingly become her favorite opponent!

The she-wolf attacked her with a stepped-up ferocity that hadn't quite been there the previous night. After all, she'd only been getting her feet wet then. With every slash and bite, it seemed as though she was working through all facets of her death-back-to-life; from her murder by Robert to this, her manifestation as a werewolf.

Andrea, by contrast, having been at the peak of her plan coming together, was completely unready for it all going utterly sideways on her so quickly. She battled back as best she could, but was wholly unprepared for the quick turn of events.

Now, roughly back to full strength with sundown, *I* broke my bonds through the fire to join my companions to quell this farce. It would be my job to turn the broken wills of the people back around from Andrea's compulsions. And who better to do it than I, ***her** maker,* to override the damage she'd done. As Emily helped set Kate back on her feet and Erika continued to wrestle with my progeny, I hauled Jones into my face and pronounced, "Fool of a lawman, this ends now! This usurper has no place here, and in no wise has she *any* authority over these citizens – or *you!* Please get their attention for me, constable; this tide needs to be turned around now!"

While he did, I turned to double check on everyone else – and they were all doing fine. Emily and Kate had gone to join the fray, utilizing some strange spell cast against Andrea. Though night *had* indeed fallen, there remained just a few faint splinters of light, as when the sky is that darkest shade of blue before it all goes black. Somehow, the witches were casting to draw out those final glints of light, magnifying them in a single beam that shone right upon my scion, weakening her ever more in her struggle against Erika. She was all alone against the three. I almost felt sorry for her – but I had the business of cleaning up her mess to attend to.

"People of Clarksville, hear *me,* the one who's served you many a night in your tavern!" I shouted out emphatically, emphasizing myself over the one who'd previously controlled them. "Let this settlement *not* be known as another Salem, adding yet another dark stain to this country's legacy. She who led you to witness and promote this action is the one who threatens this town, *not* they. Emily and Kate Laydon are honest and reliable people to this community, *not* witches. And there is *no* wolf creature about, now subduing your Jezebel, just a precious Indian daughter to one of your own!" I needed them all to *believe* that nothing presently happening was strange or amiss, least of all two witches and a werewolf teaming up against a vampire.

Ironically, at that moment as I'd referenced Jed, *he* himself appeared suddenly amongst us with Robert in tow. The sight of this wasn't going to play out well in front of the crowd, seeing him like that. One last bit of compelling to attend to then. "Robert and Jed!" I exclaimed. "Dear brothers, reunited once more!" I was laying it on almost as thick as Andrea before me. "And *you,* dear townsfolk of Clarksville, in *this* – we've come unto a *private* family affair. As such, you are dismissed, and I bid you all good night." There was pause amongst them, uncertainty; so Jones and his deputy moved in to try and get them going. Regardless, I thought it might help if I put some icing on the cake with the declaration of, "Drinks on me at the pub!" Thus, with shouts of revelry, they all finally proceeded to clear out.

With these matters attended to, I turned to see that there had come a pause on everyone else's part as well, with the advent of the brothers.

Both daughters and the mother had ceased their activities, and were staring at either Robert or Jed. I confess I did too, Robert specifically. I approached, inspecting him, all tied up. "I must say, I rather like you this way, Robert," I began, running a finger along his arm, leading to his bound wrists. "Getting into all the trouble you have with Andrea, it's good someone's finally restrained you! This actually gives me an idea insofar as my dietary needs. Some men enjoy the carnal pleasures while being 'disciplined' in this manner, do they not?"

"I suppose some deviants might, but I am not one of them, and I wouldn't know anyone such as that!" Robert replied rather emphatically. 'Doth protest too much,' crossed my mind at his answer, thus implying that he probably *did* know someone, actually. I thought also of his own bent to dominate both Emily and Kate by throwing them in the basement. I thought it curious as to what that said about him.

"What is going on here anyway?" he barked. "Better you should restrain *that* woman, than me!" he yelled, pointing his head Andrea's way.

"You have a point, Robert," I answered, turning my attention to my still reeling progeny a few paces away. "But restraint is *not* what I have in mind." Before returning to her, I looked to Jed first. "Good sir, I've come to understand that you and your daughter are hunters. Would you have a hunting knife upon you, perchance?" Though taken somewhat aback, he nodded and produced the implement and handed it to me.

"Thank you," I said.

I whirled speedily upon Andrea as Erika stepped aside from her and went to her father; giving Robert a good scare from her appearance with his proximity next to Jed. I leaned down to Andrea, poising the knife to her throat. *"This* is what I should have done in the first place – or just drained you dry. At least the wheel has come round so I *can* correct my mistake," I said.

As I began to press in to complete the deed, Emily, appearing then by my side, exclaimed, "No, wait! Is there no other way? *You* opted for another solution when I didn't care *what* you might do to my father, and you *know* what direction I was leaning."

"This is different," I replied.

"How is it different?" she blasted. "He made me, you made her. I've done things *he* doesn't approve of; *she's* done the same to you. To *all* of us, for God's sake! But, is there no room for forgiveness? That is what *you'd* have for Father and I, yes?"

"I – " I stuttered.

"Good God, woman!" Andrea exclaimed suddenly. "This has always been your problem, Charissa. Hesitation! Just do it – as you should have done intimately with James!"

Then, next to me on my other side, appeared Erika, slipping her clawed hand over mine which held the knife. "My cousin is correct – and not. *This* must be done," she spoke with uncanny clarity as she pressed our hands downward, penetrating. "But, we do this in the spirit of the hunt, not with malice to the creature who's life we take; but we do it for the good of the tribe. We forgive her as we would the bear who came upon our camp, who would seek to eat *us,* rather than we, him."

Andrea gurgled as lifeblood was pouring out; we were roughly

halfway through to total decapitation, which was what was required. With her free claw, Erika brought Emily's hand over where the two of ours already lay, not so much to help to the task, but to bring the forgiveness element she'd voiced, into it. She hesitated, squeamish at first, but then settled in, as if a memory had come to her, and she understood.

And there we were, *the witch, the wolf, and the vampire* – working together for the good, ending the abomination of my own doing; something *I* was eventually going to need to forgive *myself* for. To that end, Erika's next words poured over us like the blood pool staining the ground around Andrea's now completely severed head. "Let us take Charissa's prodigal child and offer her to Mother Earth and the Holy Father of the Heavens, that she may be atoned."

That last utterance shocked me, suddenly, to my core. She had said 'Holy Father,' as in God of Heaven and earth, as well as 'atonement.' To my knowledge, this was not a part of the Native belief system. I had prayed earlier for the advent of the Holy Ghost to us, and it had clearly come upon *her,* in revelation. There was no other explanation.

Moreover, she was speaking fluidly *in **this** form* – *another* trademark of the Spirit, whereas last night she'd been unable to vocalize whatsoever. In this, I quickly realized that the time was ripe, *right **now,*** to initiate the addition I'd suggested for the spell-cast to return her fully to normal.

"God bless you, Erika," I said. "Now – let us attend to *you,* dear girl."

• • • •

Chapter 37
Em-Erika

I t wasn't over, the *entire* process of Andrea's death and offering to above they'd made on her behalf; but the time to move onto Erika's situation was now. Or at least, Charissa seemed to think so. Emily didn't disagree when approached about it. Kate came to their side as well, as soon as she understood what was being prepared to be done.

Typically, once Robert could see what was about to happen, he balked. "You finally do something right, that *had* to be done, ending that thing, and now you go back to your sorcery."

To this, Charissa was quick to get back up in his face, scolding, *"That thing* which you allowed yourself to be beguiled by, leading you to turn against even your own family. *I,* on the other hand, never took undue advantage of you, when I easily could have. All I ever sought to do was to show you this, what we're about to try and do again. An attempt that if successful, and *you* witness, just might ease your miserable conscious. So, shut up, keep your opinions to yourself, and *do not* interfere." She looked at Jed then, concluding, "And gag him if he can't keep his mouth shut." She thought about *that* for a moment, and combined with her previous thoughts as to his restraint, it produced a wide grin across her face and a lick of her lips. Again, something for later.

Presently, Emily was running through the concept of what they sought to do with Erika, and that this time, there would be a co-mingling of the vampire and wolf blood as part of the spell. The main purpose for which being that Charissa was a believer. The theory was that, in so being, the element of *her* blood, representing Christ's resurrective ability, could somehow, *supernaturally* push Erika's metamorphosis to fruition as human, thus 'back to life,' so to speak. Erika nodded in agreement, and, with the rest of them, was ready to proceed.

Robert muttered to Jed, "Look at them, will you – my wife and daughter, *your* daughter presumably, under all that fur, and that damn Brit 'barmaid' – all mixed up together, conspiring with the Devil for God knows what."

"Brother, she already warned you, and now I am too. Shut it or I get the gag. Hell, I might punch you again another time or two if you don't watch your mouth!"

Robert at last gave in to the wisdom which he claimed to know from God – and kept quiet.

They stood in a circle, the four; two witches, one wolf and one vampire, all holding hands. Emily began, *"By sun and moon, by dark and light, may Father and Son return Erika this night."*

Em then directed Erika and Charissa to take one another's hands, each holding the other. *"From whence came dam to stop the flood, may now the turn complete by blood."* She then nodded to them as if to say, *'take, drink.'*

Charissa started first as she was the one more accustomed to regular 'feeding' in this manner. She took the clawed hand she held to her mouth and bit the wrist. It wasn't as soft or pliable as human flesh; she had to bite a little harder penetrate, and the taste, once blood was drawn, was pungent to her.

Seeing it modeled for her, Erika proceeded to take a bite into Charissa as well. It was far sweeter to her than she had been to the vampire. But this wasn't about how one tasted to the other, it was about the element produced from the bites.

Emily stepped forward, pressing their blood-stained wrists together, twisting and mushing them tightly against one another. Looking at Charissa, she said, *"By Christ whom through your veins flow, revert the native we've come to know."* Having gotten a handful of the mixture into her own palm as well, Em clasped her mother's hand with it also; from which they both began the gestures of casting.

To this, Robert murmured his displeasure, which only served to earn him an elbow into his ribs from Jed.

As the witchs' hands and arms whirled and swirled, Charissa's and Erika's touching wrists moved up to where their hands clasped again. And it was in that moment when Chris felt the shape of the hand she held to be less claw-like. Within her grasp, she slowly felt less fur and more flesh. She felt talons recede into shorter, smoother nails. Tougher, resilient skin became softer, more supple.

Taken by this, she looked into Erika's eyes, and saw a warmer, calmer brown hue coming forth. Canine protrusions of longer ears and snout regressed to normal human lobes and nose, respectively. Matted tresses became gorgeous, flowing dark hair. Trademark toned Indian skin shone brilliantly, reflecting edges in the moonlight. Charissa had disdained the time back when Andrea had come on to her; but she had to admit, in *this* moment, that **Erika** *was* beautiful. Perhaps even more so by way of being witness to such a transformation; as well as seeing Erika, actual, up close for the very first time.

During this process, Erika had dropped to her knees, her body shuddering in response to the metamorphosis. Charissa had done likewise, keeping a level position, continuing to hold her now human and – *smaller* – hand? *Was she dreaming?* Charissa wondered. She looked up from Erika's hand, to her arm, then the rest of her body; she wasn't done changing yet. She was – growing younger. Little by little, she went from a young girl, to pre-teen – to child, before her very eyes.

Shocked, Charissa pulled away, only to feel the light touch of another's hand upon her shoulder, in passing. Emily brushed past her, continuing on to Erika. Em appeared smaller and child-like as well. She went to her cousin and hugged her fiercely. Then, breaking their lengthy clinch, they stroked one another's faces like the blind might in assessing a person in order to identify them. They smiled brightly at each other, giggling like the little girls they'd become. Suddenly, they turned to go and run together towards the forest. They pranced, holding hands, blissfully moving on as if this were another time, another place.

Charissa, befuddled, turned to see Robert *with* Kate, no longer with his hands tied behind his back; *one* of them taking his wife's hand. They were smiling at one another; so too was Jed at an Indian woman who had appeared – *his* wife, presumably. Considering all that had been happening prior to this, it all seemed too perfect to be true. Charissa stood transfixed as the two couples disappeared likewise into the woods, following their daughters' lead.

She remained in her hesitancy, unsure of whether to follow and continue observing or not. She glanced down towards Andrea's severed head, wondering if she should just stand pat in hopes of resolution to her own lingering guilt over her progeny. She crouched down, brushing her fingers through Andrea's blood-matted hair. Inexplicably, Nashoba then emerged by her side, nudging the head her way as if prompting her to take it. With a heavy sigh, she took it into her hands, maneuvering it around between her palms a bit. Nashoba howled, rearing his head up and proceeded towards the tree line, a clear enough invitation for her to come along. She stood, tucked Andrea's head under her arm, and dashed after the wolf.

.

Chapter 38

Charissa

I made my way through the grove of pines until the next clearing, following Nashoba's lead all the while. As I came upon the outlying meadow, I felt as though I were entering a different dimension; a past that, in a perfect world, *should've* been, but in reality, never was. I beheld the girls frolicking about with one another, with *both* sets of parents lingering about *together*. I had come to know that all of this never occurred – it was an idyllic scene of what *could have been* without prejudice, fear, and secrets.

By now, Nashoba had gone on ahead to join them, secure that he'd done his job as my guide to get me this far. The rest was up to me, to come forth or remain an observer. As I stood there basking in the bliss before me, I noticed the burden under my arm had grown lighter. I looked, and Andrea's head was gone. Her *hand,* attached to a body without a decapitated crown clasped mine as she asked, "Walk with me, my friend?"

I gasped as tears welled up and flowed freely out of my eyes. Unlike what was happening in front of us, *this **was** us* from a time which *did* actually happen. When we *were* friends – before hurt and betrayal – and turning. I squeezed her hand back and said, "Yes, of course."

I suspect it must have been the setting – this altered state where the young cousins knew each other *in person* – which set me at ease in holding Andrea's hand – making it something innocent and playful, not too intimate or wrong. She sensed my initial hesitation, but eased up as I settled into it. "Good," she said. "None of those 'conscience hang-ups' here. Like the ones that led you to go on 'that mission from God,' in the first place."

"The mission of corrupt men," I replied.

"Exactly. But none of that in this place, see? Nothing but the uninhibited presence of love and light and laughter."

"The way **their** lives **should** have been."

"The way **our** lives **were**. And you're here to remember **that,** not how things just ended. Yes, this place is not so far removed from reality that it does not know what's occurred there. It knows, but it doesn't care. Go to them, test it out."

Taking her prompt, I moved forward, gravitating to young Emily. I hated to interrupt the cousins' time together, but I just had to jump in. I extended my arm to her and said, "Hello, Emily, do you know who I am?"

"Of course, you're Chrissa, silly," she said, grabbing my lingering arm and rubbing it to her cheek. "You're my friend!"

She knew this somehow, even as a child, who never knew me at this age. My heart cracked and my soul sang. "Can **my** friend come join us?" I asked her.

"Andra?" she confirmed as she saw her approaching. "Of course. We had our little fight with her, but we're alight now!"

Amazing. I always knew I'd like Em, but like this, as the child version, I realized how endeared to me she'd become. I pulled her in for a ferocious hug. We lingered in our clinch for a moment; and as I held her, I saw Kate and Robert waving to me some paces away. I disengaged from Em while waving back, smiling – and they to me. Surreal, utterly surreal.

I turned to see Erika had already busied herself another few meters away, ironically play-*wrestling* with Andrea, while Jed and his wife were laughing to their frolic. What she'd said was right – this place *knew* what happened in the real world; and not only didn't it care – it laughed at it, making it right and beautiful all at once.

I had to see more. I moved towards the play-fighting 'combatants,' to go and greet Erika. They growled and grunted at each other as they tossed to and fro, mimicking the real battles they'd had – elsewhere. She parted from her fun with Andrea to stop and embrace me. Andrea moved off with a light caress across my shoulder, as if in farewell.

"Chrissa," said Erika, holding me tight. Loosening her grip, her hand slid into mine.

Suddenly, there we were in the same stance and position we'd been in when the spell was cast returning her to human form. I held the hand of the young woman once again. I looked her over to make sure I wasn't still dreaming, and sure enough, she knelt against me, a grown girl, no longer a wolf hybrid and no longer dead. She smiled intuitively with brightening eyes, confirming we'd truly *been* on this little journey together.

The question now was, had only we two experienced the shift, or had the rest of them been pulled into our space as well? The answer was quickly forthcoming as the others huddled up to us, they too still reeling in a permeable afterglow. Emily was basically courteous, but nonetheless unrelenting as she pushed past me to melt fully into her cousin. I was only too happy to step aside, giving Kate a heartfelt hug hello as I let the cousins have their moment. Kate was childsplay, we had no issues between us. The biggest and most important question mark was Robert. I prayed like the dickens that he'd not only experienced this collective consciousness, but moreover been *affected* by it, softening his hardened heart. I would have to wait a moment as he turned to his wife first and foremost.

He embraced her tightly, with a hand-tapping rhythm upon her shoulder, repeating over and over, "I'm so, so sorry." Definite progress I had to say.

Releasing her, he turned to me, almost squaring himself to say his piece. "Charissa," he stated plainly in a stark pause of emphasis. "I'll not concede that you refrained from working your trickery upon me. You *did*. But I see now that, all along, your intent was pure. Unlike that 'offspring' of yours. And she played upon the hardened parts of my soul like a virtuoso. But ultimately, you did the right thing in ending her, and I'm glad to see you've had resolution with her as well. Just as I must resolve for my behavior – my sins – towards my daughter and her ways. Were it *not* for them, however misguided they might be, they've somehow brought back a life which I ended. She's given me redemption to that."

"So, go to her," I said. "That was ever and always my intention, that you two reconcile. I apologize to you *all* that my 'offspring,' as you call her, muddled things up so terribly. Which, of course, is my fault for 'making' her in the first place. That she'd follow me across the Atlantic I could never have dreamed. But, as you pointed out, I am at peace with that, with *her* now – thanks to whatever it is happened to us all by way of that spell. I believe that when we invoked Christ into it, He took *over* the spell, casting His own powers of love, forgiveness and omni-presence into it. I mean, we literally engaged into a different, better timeline, for God's sake!"

Getting his own two cents in, Jed agreed with a "You bet we did! I only wish Tanyee *was* actually here to have seen it. Speaking of which, I want to get back to our village before the night's out, so she can see Erika before she reverts back to wolf form at the end of the evening's full moon."

"Oh, that's right!" I exclaimed. "In the beauty of these moments, I forgot about that."

Apparently overhearing the conversation, Erika re-appeared into our midst, addressing her father and me. "Yes Inki, you are right, we should go. And we should take Charissa with us, as we need to prepare proper burial and ascendance for Andrea as well."

To everyone's shock, Robert said, "We should *all* go."

My oh my, if there were ever a sign that God had intervened, *that was it.*

• • • •

Chapter 39

Em-Erika

Emily stood side-by-side with her father, holding his hand even as they stood next to the little hill where she'd spell-cast before. This time it was Erika, Tanyee and Charissa who made preparations. The first order was arrangement of Andrea's head in alignment to her body, then proper directional positioning in accordance to tribal beliefs for moving on the dead.

As they watched, Emily commented to Robert, "I *never* could have dreamed, after all these years, that we'd *all* be here together – and especially not you."

"It was all *because* of that dream, daughter," he replied. "It showed every one of us what we needed to see – and learn."

"Was it just a dream though, Father? I mean, it was so real, so fluid, not like a dream at all. What if, as Charissa said, we stepped into a different version of time?"

"That's enough, Em," Kate began, whisking her away from Robert. "I told you long ago, we don't get into conversations like this with your father. Talk of things like alternate timelines are for such as we, not him," she chuckled in conclusion.

He could have been insulted had Robert not agreed with her, as he laughed robustly with her too. Soon, all three Laydons were hysterical.

Suddenly, Tanyee took charge of the moment, electing Jed to go and get 'his family' settled down. "Sorry all, my wife says the time for laughing's over. Time to get serious in laying Charissa's friend to rest."

Charissa's friend. Mere hours ago, no one would have been putting Andrea in those terms. But that was before *the turn*. Not just Erika's, though that was the crux of the matter initially. In the end, it 'turned' *everyone* who was present, taking them all into an extraordinary existential experience you couldn't help but walk away from changed. So changed too, their attitudes towards one who had been enemy, now counted as friend. It was strange to be thinking that way, but they'd all been there – heard it, seen it, felt it. And now there was simply no way *not* to let the grudge go.

No one felt this more than Charissa, standing front and center to Andrea's body, with Tanyee and Erika flanking her on either side. She was pensive, caught between a maker having sacrificed her scion here, and the girl who'd gotten her friend back over there. "I don't know what all your burial procedures consist of, my ladies, but I recommend, inasmuch as we *are* vampires, that we burn Andrea as we did Erika in preparation for the spell before. I'm not here to tell you what to do in your land, it's just my sage advice."

Tanyee nodded, then Erika back to her, as if perhaps they'd already had this in mind. On that very note, she lit the little pyre they'd gathered round the dead Andrea. Erika took over from there to speak the words as she had more familiarity with the vampire, having battled with her twice. "Friend who was foe and who is comrade once more,

we lay you down to raise you up. You were our ally's friend before she came here, and even while things went awry, you were an honorable opponent. You went too far and we had to stop you for the good of all, and now *all* are with you. Journey well to Earthly Mother and Heavenly Father, dear Andrea."

That said, Tanyee and Erika tossed beans and corn into the consuming fire as was their custom.

After they'd finished, Charissa asked, "Are there any bodies of water in the vicinity where I might scatter the ashes? Like myself, Andrea loved the Thames in London."

"The Cumberland River isn't too far," Tanyee offered. I can take you there once you've gathered the ashes. But the night grows short, perhaps later in the day?"

"I cannot go unless under cover of night. Perhaps one of my witches would care to cast for me a sun shield spell once more?"

"Of course, Charissa," Kate and Emily answered in unison, then giggled as they caught themselves.

"Very well, thank you," concluded Charissa.

• • • •

As Tanyee had alerted, the night was moving towards dawn, so the lot of them decided it was time to return to their village from the hill. It would be a cold day in hell as the coming dawn would see Robert Laydon as a guest – in an Indian camp. Not to mention a vampire, two witches, and their own 'wolf'!

Respectively, one witch and the wolf girl conversed amongst themselves as the group walked. "Did you know all what would

happen when you cast that spell, Em?" Erika asked pointedly.

"You mean, what happened beyond turning you back human again?" answered Em. "No, not at all! That was *not* my spell. I think Charissa got it right when she said our invocation of Jesus into the cast saw *Him* take it over somehow."

"I believe that," Erika returned. "Just like I believe this Christ you ascribe to showed *me,* even before that, that He is there, *with* Spirits of Earth and Sky, yet *over* them."

"I remember when you said that. I was surprised, because I didn't think you recognized the Father and the Son in your culture."

"We do not – normally. But in the midst of all our strange turmoil, I was *shown.* And now I see that there is more than just what we believe."

"Don't go utterly abandoning your beliefs though, cousin. Your people have a reverence and understanding of God *through* His creations such as earth, sky, and water that we of Christian faith often fail to respect."

"That is because, as so many before you, your people are convinced that they are 'ordained' of God to *conquer* and *take* the land for their own control of it, rather than embrace it, becoming one with it, as we do."

"You're right, that's what I like about it," agreed Em. "Come to think of it, all the while we've been growing up, there's been the war with Charissa's people, fighting for our own freedom, only to be looking to encroach upon your territories at the same time. It's not right."

"No, it's not. And I fear it will get worse before it gets better. My inki wasn't sent here to fall in love, you know; it was as an emissary from

your government to peacefully placate us. I fear for him if the time comes that they try to remove us. For, he was never meant to stay as he has."

"You think they'll try to push you out?"

"I'd not be surprised. It's been done already, here and there. This land of Tennessee once had many more tribes than it does now. Presently, only we and the Cherokee remain. But, we are skilled negotiators; we'll find a way to get ahead of it."

"That's good. As it is, though, I'm glad our settlers landed here, and Jed wound up going to you. I'm proud to be a friend of the tribe and cousin to you. Even though we were robbed of our childhood together, we're blessed to have seen what it would have been like tonight!"

"Yes – we thought it would just be returning me to normal, but we got so much more!"

"I'm sorry that the spell will only allow you to be back this way sometimes, and not always."

"It's all right, Em – you forget how bonded I am into Nashoba; how much we believe in the communion with animals even *before* that took place. I count it as honor to be such a being. Do not fret about it."

As passing time had yet to reveal, the spell cast designed to bring Erika back *only* during full moon phase would prove to be enhanced by the Holy Spirit's integration into the spell. In the weeks and months to follow, human Erika came to manifest *anytime* the moon was visible, in any and all phases of the Earth's lone satellite, much to the delight of her family and the tribe. But other things of her future would not be so kind.

* * * *

The next day, the four women and the he/she wolf made their trek to the Cumberland River for Charissa to scatter Andrea's ashes. The somber vampire was lightened somewhat for the fact that, within her company of supernaturals, she was *able* to do this. In the day, in the light. With the aid of her witch sisters, she could make this journey feeling the warmth of the morning sun upon her face and body, as she carried the pottery jar of her friend's remains.

She approached the banks of this river unknown to her. Still, a river it *was*. In her mind, she simply went back to the Thames and pretended she was there, with Andrea too. Making sure she was inclined enough to make a good toss, she uncapped the lid of the crafted jar and with a good roundhouse arc of her arm, scattered the ashes into the light breeze, which carried them gently onto the water's surface. She said nothing other than, "Forgive me," as the water moved

Andrea into its current. Within her imagination, she thought of the ashes being carried from the river to the mouth of the North Sea.

As Emily and NashErka came to her side, Charissa turned to Tanyee and asked, "Where does this river lead?"

"To my knowledge," she replied, "it meanders to the south into Louisiana and the Gulf of Mexico; and going northward, it snakes greatly and diminishes, never quite reaching the great Lake Michigan of Illinois."

"I should like to see this 'great lake,' of the north one day I think," Charissa answered, imagining *her* North Sea.

"But you're staying here for now, yes?" queried Emily, while Nash craned his/her head in curious canine fashion.

"For now, yes, I believe I will. I've journeyed far and been blessed to find people such as you and your cousin; 'creatures' more like myself. I'd be a fool to have found you, then leave. When the wanderlust comes, I shall heed it. Until then, I shall enjoy 'my time in the sun' with you," Charissa joked.

The witches laughed in response, and in short order everyone was giggling. And in the tone of a laugh, NashErka howled.

The
Coming
Years

Chapter 40
Charissa

As promised, I stayed in Clarksville many more years, decades even. I hadn't been jesting when I'd talked of having found a 'family.' With Emily's aid in accompaniment, with sun protection spell-casts, I would venture with her, revisiting the cousins' rendezvous of old in between their lands – to go hunting with the wolf. I'd committed to not procuring all of my nourishment from available humans; I needed to balance it by going into the wild with some regularity. Hunting with NashErka was a unique bonding experience for us; we got to know each other very well through the teaming of our predatory activity. When the days were done and our kills made, I would excuse myself when the moon came up in order to give the cousins alone time together, once Erika would return to her original self.

The passing of time saw Emily and Erika (when she was human), become beautiful young women. Their mothers and fathers began to push towards elderly, while I – I remained the same. Sometimes you don't learn *all* about what you've become right away. Apparently, as a vampire, I wasn't going to age normally, if at all. I wondered if other whispered lore was true also; that I would outlive *this* group of people, and many other generations to come? Time would tell.

Time would also bring trials and travesty which would change us all, and mostly *not* for the better. Just as the Americans had battled for their independence against my people prior to my arrival, now *they* too decided to wage a 'quiet' war against the native peoples. This occurred some thirty years later, but had been building towards it for much of that time. There was no formal declaration of war, mind you, simply an 'act' of Congress, they called it. The kind of act that generally *does* occur after a war's been waged and won; the taking of a conquered peoples' domain. America wanted their lands for growth and 'progress'; preferred prime territory for advancement of the country, while moving the tribes into less desirable, sub-par areas.

This affected us all greatly inasmuch as our neighboring Chickasaw family were, of course, a direct target. There was little we could do to try and stop it, and it would've been a misguided effort to do so regardless. Unlike most other native tribes, the Chickasaw chiefs were well-versed in the art of negotiation. They skillfully brokered land deals with the U.S. and even had the foresight to *schedule* their migration during the seasons when the weather was more favorable. Unfortunately, this didn't alleviate any and all casualties brought on by their trek hundreds of miles through wilderness to Oklahoma. The Chickasaw still suffered deaths; and specifically, Erika's family lost a grandfather *and* both her parents in the process.

It wasn't that Jed and Tanyee were *so* aged that they'd not been up for the journey; no, there'd simply been some health problems, but were fully manageable. An unexpected storm front on the way had

been the catalyst for catching pneumonia, which took down Tanyee before they'd made it to their destination. Jed had survived, but remained weakened in both mind and body. In his pain over the loss of his wife, he passed one night in his sleep, probably dreaming of going to join her.

Erika was devastated at this, as Emily and myself would come to learn when we traveled ourselves to see her, sadly, after the fact. Em became privy to this knowledge through her continued dream-walks with her cousin, though choppy at that great a distance. I chided myself as I'm apt to do, for not going with them in the first place, to perhaps have helped more in some way. To be fair though, it had seemed they'd had the situation well in-hand, and we'd simply wished them well, sending prayers for a safe journey. After all, *I'd* navigated across an ocean to get here. How could we have known?

What we *did* come to know – when Em and I finally arrived to visit – was that Erika had become bitter and reclusive, having removed herself from the community. As it turned out, the passing of time had turned the general attitude of the tribe towards her, from beloved to suspect. The creature she'd become, *combined* with the trauma caused by the Removal, had become something of a bad omen to the people; and they'd come to connect the two. Idiots.

Erika had been by no means forced out, however. When we found her, with directional help from a chieftan, she would later explain how she *herself* had come to feel out of place and isolated in her grief. She'd left of her own accord, moody and better off alone. This was clear as crystal the day we located her at last – her wolf self was aggressive even to *us,* her closest friends. My guess was, from the long time apart,

she and Nash weren't exactly seeing it that way presently. And there, within the Oklahoma hillside, I thought I was going to have to revisit my first encounter with Erika's wolf-self, once more having to do battle with the she-beast.

Chapter 41
Em-Erika

Charissa snarled at NashErka while making herself 'big,' trying to assert dominance, but it wasn't working. The pitch of the wolf's growls continued to rise as if in warning that a lunge was forthcoming. It might've been, but Emily stepped in and did the very opposite of what Charissa had. She knelt down, submissive, only gently calling out their names, "Nashoba – Erika. I'm here. *We're* here. We should have been sooner; probably should've gone with you all in the first place, and I'm sorry. I know our dream connection hasn't been good – you've fallen off, grown distant. I barely knew what was happening, but I could tell it was dark – bad. I knew we had to come."

In her head, Emily heard Erika's reply telepathically from within the wolf, *"It's about time."*

Later, when night had fallen and Nashoba had become Erika again, she spoke to them freely, verbally. "So, what do you think? I'm a 'lone wolf' now, out in the wilderness, separate from the tribe. I felt so lost without my parents, being away from the land that *was* ours, and being away from the two of you. Then the whispers and the murmurs started. I'd been considered a blessed thing for many years, but after the migration, they began looking at me as a bad omen, that perhaps I'd brought upon them a curse, for being what I am, and then what happened. Between that and missing my parents so, I couldn't stay any longer and came out here."

"I'll *show* them a real curse if they want one," Charissa began spouting, her old default of 'vampire vengeance' rearing its head. "I'm happy to add another tribe to the one already on my ledger, for it sounds as though they need an attitude adjustment!"

"It sounds to me like *you* need one right now, Chris," Emily replied cutting her off. "Settle down and leave her tribe be. I don't think it's what she or God would want, right Erika?"

"No, I wouldn't want that at all," she replied. "Though I'd like to tell you what I *do want,* dear cousin. Something only you can do..."

"Of course, anything."

"Do you think you could reverse the spell tying my spirit to Nashoba?"

"Excuse me? Are you asking what it sounds like?"

"Yes, I am. I have cheated death and garnered many extended years of life by what we did, and I am grateful. I have loved being tied in unison to my wolf, and the union I've shared with you and Charissa. But things are different now. My tribe shuns me, and those I wish most to be with have passed to the realm where I've already been, and now I wish to return to it, and to them."

"Oh my goodness," Emily blanched, moving forward to hug her cousin. "Are you sure? What of Nash? You've been bonded for so long, you'll be leaving within him a great hole in the place where *you* were."

"I will aid with that," Charissa interrupted. "We'll continue to hunt together as we have; I will be there to help him through his loss. And you will too, Emily, you are another of his familiars. He'll be all right, we'll make sure of it," she concluded, painfully smiling at Erika.

Em pulled back from her clinch with Erika, looking her dead in the eyes. "You realize in asking this of *me,* you complete the circle that started with my father, who took your life in the first place, yes? You have a cruel sense of irony, cousin."

"Perhaps it is also *fitting,* Em," Erika replied. "You played God, in a sense, bringing me back. More to the point, *played* Jesus, if you think about it! Now I simply ask that you return the control of life and death back to the One who authors it."

To which, Emily could find no further basis for debate. "How did you become so wise in the ways of God, cousin? Not bad – for an Indian! Next thing you know, you'll be telling me how I should abandon magic altogether, just *like* my father would, speaking of him!"

"I *will not,* not like him. Magic is a wonderful thing; all humans, natives and settlers alike, wish to touch it, feel its workings. I am living proof. But I've heard it said that 'magic has its price,' and perhaps this is why God would have us steer more clear of it?"

"Perhaps. I wouldn't have listened to this attitude when we were younger, when I wielded it with confidence and prowess. And besides, Father, in his dominance, pushed me towards it; when I *needed* its strength in rebellion against his cruel ways. Now, not so much."

"As you once told me, 'don't abandon my beliefs utterly,' hang on to what is good," added Erika.

"Yes," Charissa chimed in once more, "do not go renouncing your craft on me while I am still in need of daylight protection, please!"

The three of them chuckled at this, and before long were laughing hysterically; a needed break to the seriousness which was before them. When they'd finally settled down and sat, Emily looked at both of them with her final answer to the request at hand which she technically, had not yet given.

"I have done very few reversal spells in my time, but for you, cousin, I will try. I do so with great remorse, but, more than anything, I want you to be happy – and I understand. However, I have a request of my own first. Before you're gone from us, Erika, we should all have together

– one

– last

– hunt.

Epilogue
Charissa

'The last hunt,' as it were, came to be that which Emily had hoped for. One thing I always liked about Em was that she was precise. She didn't want this little hunt of hers to be just over and done with. No, she had stipulations. Erika had to return with us to the Tennessee territory (thereby extending our time together), and the exercise *had* to be in the woods where they'd sneak away to find each other as youths. I didn't at all disagree with her either – it's where my memories of hunting with Nashoba lay too; and I would have many more with him *without* Erika's presence in the future.

As it was, our hunt was in the night, fittingly, when supernaturals roam! The reason being, Em wanted this last time with her cousin to be with *her*, in human form, not the wolf. We would have plenty of that in the days to come after Erika had left us. Both girls – hurmph! Both *women* were grown adults now, and utilized the bow and arrow – a

gun too loud to be ringing off shots under cover of dark. I, of course, bore no weapon, using only my fangs, strength, speed and stealth. It was glorious – I'd been blessed beyond measure to have found these two, in their own ways, like me; at least the 'me' I was now. I would dearly miss the she-wolf, but we still had 'just-the-wolf' in her wake, and I think he always had a residue of her remaining, somewhere deep inside.

So, *yes,* the reversal spell releasing the tethered souls of wolf and woman together *was* ultimately successful, and Erika passed on as she had originally, some thirty-odd years ago. As with 'the last hunt,' this would be the last *major* spell Emily would cast. She'd taken to heart 'the price of magic,' and that it might not be a practice quite 'ordained of God,' so to speak. She came to feel that, though the *power* of magic was definitely a glimpse into what's possible with God in his realm beyond here, there was a limit on how much we should 'play' with it. I assume she felt she'd reached that limit. I couldn't argue that – finding a way to bring someone back to life *was* fairly high up that scale!

As such, Emily weaned me off of daylight protection magic, and I regressed back into being a 'creature of the night.' That is when I'd go hunt with Nash;

and when I began experimenting with the men at the pub in more 'restraining' ways of extra-curricular activities, finding it to be extremely well-suited to attain my dietary needs, at least when I chose human nourishment.

Emily and I by no means had gone separate ways; I'd be with her even unto her days as a withered, old woman. But, as she backed off more and more from magic, she became less and less my supernatural counterpart; while I, by contrast, couldn't choose. I was, and would

continue to be the thing that I am, far past these decades. She would always be more spiritual than religious, but she did, ultimately circle back towards a more traditional belief system. The little magic she did keep practicing was more esoteric; applying healing applications in nature, wounded animal rescues, and tending to the sick.

Never did I begrudge her, but I'd become less given over to *full* trust in faith, the direction she had gone. I'd come to merely trust God to do what he will; not necessarily *always* looking out for everything and everyone. And certainly *not* in terms of this 'Christian Nation' that was forming. Though the morality was basically sound, what it had done both with slaves and to the native peoples certainly wasn't 'what Jesus would do,' I'm sorry. And when it had struck so personally to *us,* well, let us just say, I wasn't in a 'forgiving' place. At least, not as yet, and not for a long time to come.

Presently, I was on a path of building loss upon loss, which wasn't good soil for the seed planting of abounding faith. Obviously, Erika was gone along with her parents, as were Emily's now too, and Nash had grown so old he couldn't hunt anymore at all. Only Em and I remained, and as the waning years of her life set in, I began to set my sights to the north, where I'd learned a young, promising city had sprouted upon the shores of the great lake spoken of by Tanyee.

"The wanderlust has set into you at long last, Charissa," Emily said to me one day. "I can see it in your eyes. You should go, prosper in Chicago."

"And leave you to die alone?" I asked as though affronted. "I think not."

"I'm not alone, I have Nash."

"Who should be long dead by now, as should I. Ahh, magic, curses and their price!"

"I'm sorry I was unable to do anything to undo the dark magic that holds you in its lock, Charissa. You know I tried, but undoing another's work is different than undoing your own."

"I understand. But unfortunately, this curse is tied as much to physical chemistry as it is magic, so I'm pretty well stuck I fear."

"'Stuck' as a beautiful woman," Em reminded, "what I wouldn't give to be as you again."

"You could do magic."

"I could, but no more cheating – youth nor death. God shall soon have his due."

"I could *make* you as I am, but if we were to have done that, it should've been when youth remained!"

She cackled a boisterous laugh to that; we both did actually. Still supernatural or not, I would miss this, miss her. Emily would always be magic to me, even if she no longer practiced. But she didn't, and in a few short years, she would be gone altogether, and my journey through this country would continue again. To the 'windy city' upon the great lake I would go, and try to build a new life in the wake of the one I'd be sadly leaving behind.

"A priest," old lady Laydon interrupted in the middle of my muse.

"What?" I asked.

"A priest," she repeated. "You should go to Chicago and find yourself one. You used to admire them."

"Excuse me, but for what purpose?"

"To restore you your faith," she concluded, patting my hand.

* End *

A .F. Roberts was raised in Phoenix, Arizona by transplants from Chicago. As a youth, comic books and science-fiction were major influences. High School through college brought an introduction to Christianity, which, combined with the former, birthed not only a refreshment of spirit, but also an imagination enhanced by stories of the bible and theological prophecy. **www.afroberts.com**[1]

Roberts studied Advertising Arts at Maricopa Tech/Gateway Community College, earning an A.A.S. degree, leading to positions in the field of community newspapers. With experience in both press operations and pre-press layout, production work occasionally resulted in photo journalism or newswriting assignments. In life, divorce and single parenting steered into journaling. In tandem, these elements began the progression into creative writing.

Roberts continues to reside in Phoenix, reading and writing books and staying close to his son. He attends Living Streams Church and maintains employment in the print industry at Short Run Printing LLC, which produces magazines, and ironically, books and comics.

---

1. http://www.afroberts.com

More by A.F. Roberts

Blood Light[2]

Charissa, the 200-year-old vampire you just read about, now lives and works in present-day, Old Town Chicago, only blocks away from the parish of Father Christopher, a dutiful Catholic priest whose only real concern is the spiritual welfare of his community. That is, until the two meet – and are never the same again.

A 'chance' meeting brings the Man of God and the Mistress of the Night into a strangely symbiotic relationship – once she feeds upon him – something she initially tried hard to resist. Soon, they are sensing one another's patterns in odd daydream interludes, building towards a newfound connection neither of them can deny.

Charissa's cannibalistic vampire origins come into the picture when her maker, a cannibal shaman of the Caribbean, throws out his own tangled web in an attempt to re-connect with her after over a century of silence between them.

Christopher and Charissa find themselves, plus her friend Ariyah and her beau Joe, in the middle of a cross-continental nightmare leading them into the still cannibal-infested islands of the West Indies...

---

2. http://afroberts.com/blood-light/

The *Cross-Gate Trilogy,* **Book One; the Story that Started it All!**

The Severs are a family in turmoil. They are David, his teens Cassie and Jeff, and Carolyn, his estranged wife. David and Cassie possess latent abilities they toyed with when she was a child, dabbling unwittingly with a technique known as dream-walking.

Presently they find themselves doing it again, coinciding with dreams David is having of a circular cross shape and a Templar Knight. David's eccentricities surrounding his dream world are wreaking havoc throughout his family life. Carolyn seeks out new age church alternatives as her solution, while David is opposed.

Cassie cares little for either, but is drawn to her father's dreams, and begins to share in them. Desiring only family preservation, her brother Jeff allies with their mother and her new found mentor Murro Vogt, a charlatan leader of a church known as The Gateway. As Vogt takes the two under his wing, his true motives in engaging this family, because of their ancestry line to the Knights Templar, slowly emerge.

Cassie's allegiance to her father and his resistance towards Vogt brings the two sides towards collision course, leading to Cassie's introduction to Sandra Nikells, a psychic consultant to the police department. Nikells appears when a tragedy of Vogt's making strikes the family. She coaches Cassie and David in the art of dream walking and the use of dream gates. As these skills are honed, the mystery of David's dream cross circles become clearer. They are revealed to be gateways of cross-over passage to the other side...

Em-erika A.F. Roberts

Don't miss out!

Visit the website below and you can sign up to receive emails whenever A.F. Roberts publishes a new book. There's no charge and no obligation.

https://books2read.com/r/B-A-KIKM-HOVNB

BOOKS 2 READ

Connecting independent readers to independent writers.